Tempting Shadowed Hearts
An FFFF Monster Romance
Mikaelynn Rose

Content Warnings

- sexual activity on page

- SA on page

- minor SA off page

- pregnancy of a minor from the result of SA

- on page loss of pregnancy

- death on page

- primal play

Songs that inspired this book

- Cravin' – Stileto, Kendyle Paige

- AMERICAN HORROR SHOW – Snow Wife

- Let It Go (with Lo Spirit) – Chandler Leighton

- Watch Me – bludnymph

- I Really F**ked It Up – girli

- DARKSIDE – Neoni

- Play with Fire (feat. Yacht Money) – Sam Tinnesz

- Change – NF

- D!E FOR ME – Ekoh

- Beg (On Your Knees) – Ash to Eden

- on your knees – Ex Habit

- Slumber Party (feat. Princess Nokia) – Ash-
  nikko

- Good Enough – Lo Spirit

- Run Rabbit – ALT BLK ERA

- RUNRUNRUN – Dutch Melrose

Listen to the Playlist on Spotify

For the girls, gays and theys.
If you've never had a seat at the table, baby pull one up.
The girls are ready for you.

Contents

Prologue

Avyanna

I've dedicated the majority of my long life to protecting those who can't protect themselves, hunting the monsters who take advantage of the innocent—those human and... not. I guess the reason I'm so good at what I do is that I'm not much better than they are; it takes a monster to know a monster. The difference between them and me is that I only target the innocent when I have no choice or when I lose control of myself. In those cases, I've thanked my lucky stars that I am what I am and can blend into any crowd without rousing suspicion.

You're probably wondering how I accomplish this. What I am. Well, my kind has been called many things over the years:

Shape shifter.

Changeling.

Doppelgänger.

Imposter.

Mimic.

Skin walker.

None of these names are wrong, per se, but skin-walker is the one I hate the most. It's the one monstrous name that sparks fear in far too many people, especially those in the Appalachian region. That name is the reason I'm so cautious about who sees what I'm capable of.

Most people consider us shapeshifters. While we are shapeshifters of a sort, we don't turn into animals like ordinary shifters; we turn into other people.

The most common—and, in my opinion, accurate—names we're given are doppelgänger and mimic. Those of us who are good at what we do are able to look nearly identical to our intended person.

The only feature of my own I can't seem to part with when I change is a lone freckle on my cheekbone. My mother used to refer to it as a beauty mark. Although it's small, it's still there and can affect my desired image, clashing with the features I'm trying to imitate. Most of the time, it isn't a problem, though. I've worked hard over the years to hone my features with each change, but it doesn't matter who I try to become; that damn thing is still there. Other than that minute detail, I'm one of the best of my kind, hence why I've lived so long and am in such high demand in my field.

Now I'm sure you're wondering how old I am. Let's just say that I've walked this earth for centuries. I've traveled all over—seen every sight there is to see in this world—and I'm getting tired.

Tired of the same sights that I've seen hundreds of times.

Tired of doing the same thing over and over because there's nothing else for me to do.

Tired of being *alone.* Because that's how I've spent the majority of the last several centuries.

When I was young, someone murdered my parents, and none of my family really wanted to deal with me, so they passed me around like a sack of potatoes. After a few years, they all started dying out of nowhere, one by one. The only person left for me to live with in the end was my uncle.

At that point, I was about fifteen and had become used to bouncing from house to house. The idea of no longer having to do so was a relief, but things didn't stay that way for long. For the first month, and in the presence of others, he was the nicest man in the world. He bought me everything I could ever want, made sure I was well taken care of, and treated me like the daughter he never had.

After that first month, he became the monster I still have nightmares about. It started with hugs and touches that were more intimate than they should've been. Then, he started picking out the clothes I was to wear, choosing things that revealed more skin than I was comfortable with. When I told him how I felt, he backhanded me and told me I was lucky he even took me in..

It wasn't long after that when he came into my bedroom and started touching me. He told me he 'wanted to make me feel good.' I tried to fight him, but eventually he tied me down and forced himself upon me. The entire time, he laughed and told me he was going to 'ruin me for all other men' and was making me his forever because no man wanted a woman who'd allowed another man to touch her. I screamed until my throat was raw, but no one helped me.

This became a near-nightly occurrence for the rest of the time I lived with him.

After a few months, I started getting sick out of nowhere. I thought nothing of it at first; there was always some sort of sickness going around, and back then, we didn't know much about them. But when I missed my period, I knew something was going on. I monitored my symptoms for nearly a month before I asked a neighbor to take me to the doctor. After an examination and some now considered odd urine tests, they told me I was pregnant, and I cried the entire way home. Thankfully, my neighbor didn't ask questions.

Month by month flew by, and even with my belly and breasts growing, my uncle didn't realize anything was different. I was grateful because I had no clue what I was going to do. I didn't want to bring a child into his home, but the doctor told me my baby would be arriving soon.

Boy, was he right, just in the worst way possible. One morning, I woke up in immense pain. At the time, I wasn't sure where it was coming from, but when I got out of bed, I felt an unfamiliar slickness between my legs, so I hurried to the bathroom. Once in the light, I nearly dropped to the floor. Blood was running freely down my legs while pain like no other wrapped around my belly into my back.

My heart sank.

Something was very wrong.

When the pain subsided the first time, I did my best to clean up the mess on the floor. Then another rush of pain engulfed me, and I had to clench my teeth to avoid screaming. The last thing I wanted was for my uncle to know what was happening to me.

Of course, we didn't have phones back then, so I couldn't call anyone, but I knew I had to get checked out. I wasn't sure how I managed to get dressed and make it to my neighbor's house; I just knew I had to do it for my baby. My neighbor rushed me to the doctor, avoiding my uncle per my request, all while trying to keep her face stoic so she wouldn't scare me. Deep down, I knew the odds weren't good.

My baby—a little girl I would've done anything to keep, no matter the circumstances of her conception—died in my arms a few hours later. I wished I'd died alongside her. If it weren't for what I am, I would've because of all the blood I lost. But I didn't. I knew it was for the best that she didn't make it; it just didn't make it any easier. I just knew that the life I was forced to live wasn't suitable for a baby, especially since I was still a child myself.

When I returned home that evening, my uncle was livid because I hadn't told him where I was going. He forced me back to my room, intent on locking me in there as a punishment, but then he discovered the blood in my bed and punished me for ruining it.

Through all that, he still never did find out about my daughter.

Just after I turned sixteen, his gaze fell upon another young woman whom he quickly acquired possession of. Once she was settled in his home, he tried to sell me off to his friend, but I disappeared before he could complete the deal.

He chased me all over the country for several years before someone finally killed him, and I could lie low for a few years. Fear gripped me at the thought of venturing out because I knew there were other monsters out there just waiting to take advantage of a young woman. I refused to let them get their hands on me. Not only that, but I had to allow myself some time to heal.

After a few more years in hiding, I decided to try my hand at fitting into society again. At first, things went well. The world had changed, but it was still predominantly male-dominated. Women had absolutely no rights, so it was frowned upon for a woman to remain unmarried or be without her parents while she remained so. The biggest mistake I made during this time was allowing those around me to know what I was. I should've taken on the identity of another until I knew more about these people. But I was still young and knew nothing about society back then.

The church quickly discovered I was unmarried and orphaned. To appease society's expectations, they presented me to several bachelors and basically auctioned me off to the highest bidder. But the thought of another man touching me repulsed me, so I tried to escape several times. I made the mistake of changing my appearance, and that's when they discovered I wasn't human. Upon capturing me, they locked me in a room until my new husband came to claim me.

He was a vile man who often kept me locked in the house to keep me from leaving. It didn't keep me from trying, though. I fought him every step of the way. And when he tried to rape me, I killed him with my bare hands.

It was my first murder, but I don't regret it, even to this day. The thing that hurt the most was when I found out I wasn't his first victim by any stretch of the imagination. And the church was condoning his actions by giving him woman after woman when he was done with the last.

After the church found out what I did, they tried to lock me up again, and the townspeople lost their minds. They called me a murderer and claimed the man I killed deserved justice. Yet no one took the time to listen to me because I was a woman. Everything I'd done to that man was done in self-defense. And no one batted an eye at the fact that he had killed other women before me. Did his victims not deserve justice?

I got out of that town as quickly as possible, changing my appearance several times while I traveled to avoid recognition. When things cooled down and I actually took the time to look at everyone around me, I realized that there were more monsters than I could've ever imagined in this world. That's when I knew I had to do something. So I did what no one else would at the time; I began hunting down the monsters no one was doing anything about.

Hunting them down has slowly turned me into one of them, though. Especially when I'm on a mission and forget to feed myself. Let's just say that when I get hungry, I lose sight of who I am. It doesn't help that normal food doesn't do shit for me when I get to that point. When I'm starved, the only thing that can satisfy me is the life essence of another. Basically, I either drink blood or take a piece of someone's soul.

I hate it because I don't want to be a bad person, but when hunger takes over, I lose control. I've killed my fair share of likely decent people by accident. If it's a monster, I don't feel as bad. But that's why I let it get so damn bad sometimes. I figure that if I let myself lose control with a monster, I can justify it. I'm going to kill them either way.

When said monsters are demons, it fucks everything up, though. They can't offer me anything because they don't have souls, and their blood is toxic if ingested. So, I've learned to pace myself and keep tabs on my hunger when pursuing a demon. Thankfully, they're sparse in the human realm—they tend to stick to their own realm more often than not.

Since I'm one of the best hunters there is, I'm highly sought after. It doesn't surprise me that most know me—I've walked this damned Earth for long enough.

But hunting all these monsters doesn't feel like a purpose enough anymore. I want more from my life than just this bullshit.

Over the years, there've been several people who've made me realize that not *everyone* is awful. At least, that's how I remember them. Then again, maybe I'm just lying to myself and making those people seem better in my mind because I want some fucking meaningful interaction. A friend who won't judge me for what I am. Maybe even a little bit of love... if that's a thing for someone like me.

My problem with finding someone to fill the empty void in my life is that I struggle to see the good in others. Monsters and those who've wronged me in the past have tainted my view of society as a whole. It's as if I'm always worried that someone is out to get me. I've spoken to some of my longtime colleagues about how I'm feeling, and they tell me to rely on my instincts when I'm getting to know someone. They say it's 'what'll tell you if someone is inherently good or bad.'

I've tried trusting my instincts a few times, and I think whoever said that in the first place is full of shit. The last time I tried to 'trust my gut,' the relationship fucked me up for years. Needless to say, I'm going to put that advice on the back burner. Or I might not ever use those things again.

While I *have* become desperate for connection, I won't settle for just anything or anyone. I want someone who can keep up with my disastrous lifestyle, someone who isn't worried about being caught up in it. I need someone who can bring a little bit of light to my otherwise dark life, but also someone who's been through some shit and doesn't expect their life to be sunshine and rainbows constantly. Last, but most importantly, I want someone who isn't looking to fuck me over, mistreat me, or hurt me. There's been enough of that in my life.

I think maybe I need to change the way I look at people. And I need to *attempt* to open up to others more than I have in the past. The idea of it scares the fuck out of me, but I'm tired of being so lonely all the time.

Pain and hatred are the only things I've felt for so long, and I really want to feel something different again.

Chapter One

Avyanna

I stride across the rooftop of a two-story building, heading for a scent I know all too well, one that captures my attention no matter where I am. Blood. With the massive amounts I'm detecting, I assume I'm going to find a body, but I have to be careful. You never know if your perp has left the area until you get there.

When I approach the edge, a courtyard comes into view. It would be even more beautiful if there wasn't a dead woman who's been nearly ripped to shreds in the center. A pang of sadness echoes through me because I know I'm not here to track down a monster; I'm here for a woman.

Roxanna Emeri Marie Bellavance

Remember how I said I wanted to feel something besides pain and hatred? Well, one look at this beautiful woman nearly a century ago made me feel something different.

Obsession.

At first, I was pissed because out of all the fucking emotions, why did it have to be that one? I watched over her for nearly three weeks, trying to figure out who she was and why I was having such an intense reaction to her presence. While I watched her, my mind calmed, like some semblance of peace washed over me, which had never happened before.

But then my hunger tried to take over, and I nearly went feral, so I had to leave. When I returned, the house was empty. I was gone for all of three days. *Three fucking days.*

I've been looking for her ever since, getting tips here and there that haven't panned out. Something just feels different about this one. I'm not ready to let her go yet.

A man's voice drifts up to me from the courtyard, bringing me back to reality. "What the fuck is happening in this city? This is the third girl this week. Someone needs to stop this monster before the humans discover what's happening right under their noses."

I glance down and find a woman standing beside him. She shifts on her feet with her arms crossed over her chest, uncomfortable with the scene before her.

"With it being near Halloween, supes are already walking a fine line in this city, especially since these damn humans grow more and more suspicious by the day. There are so many stories about us supes and what we're rumored to be capable of. As much as the fuckers scare me, maybe someone should bring the hunters in."

At her mention of a hunter, I hop down into the courtyard. The man and woman startle, accidentally dropping their human glamour slightly and showing what they truly are. I already know, though. Some of us supes, myself included, can see through glamour, straight to someone's core. Just by looking at someone, I know not only what kind of supernatural they are, but I'm also able to see what kind of person they are, including the good and the bad they are capable of.

The man—a centaur—squares his shoulders and balls his fists. He has no chance against me, but I'll let him think he does. "Who the fuck are you?"

Standing tall, I roll my shoulders back and crack my neck. "I'm going to guess you guys aren't detectives of any sort because I've been up on that ledge since before you arrived, and I'm about ninety-five percent certain neither of you spotted me up there. Needless to say, I suggest you brush up on your senses to avoid being attacked in the future. Now, if you are detectives, I think I need to speak to your supervisor."

The woman—a siren—crosses her arms and furrows her brows. "First off, rude. Second, you didn't answer his question. Who are you?"

I place my hand on my chest and gasp. "You mean you can't tell just by looking at me? I actually allowed myself to be in my own skin for once! Everyone tells me my reputation precedes me, but I have a feeling they lie to make me feel better," I say. When neither acknowledges me, I let out an exasperated breath. "You're no fun. But you *are* in luck; you've found yourself a hunter. I smelled the blood of the victim over a mile away, so I came to check it out."

The centaur lets his eyes roam up and down my body. I can practically feel the skepticism rolling off him. Rarely am I the one everyone assumes would be involved in this type of work. I'm most definitely not skinny, but there's a lot of muscle underneath my curves.

Looks can be deceiving, though, especially when you can alter them.

The centaur tenses his jaw. "How do we know you're not the one who did this?"

I roll my eyes. "You'd know if I was the one to do this because my victims look nothing like this once I'm done with them."

"Interesting," the siren muses before tapping her finger on her arm. "What are you doing here? I haven't heard about any cases from nearby cities being taken over by The D.A.M.N.E.D. recently."

Okay, let me explain this really quickly. D.A.M.N.E.D. is the acronym for the organization I work for. It's short for Deathless Agents for Monster Neutralization, Erasure, and Destruction. It's a mouthful, hence why we call it The D.A.M.N.E.D. The organization has hunters all over the world, and while I may work for them, I'm more of a freelancer. I take the cases I want, not what they try to give me. I'm older than nearly all our council members, and everyone has learned over the years just to let me do what I please. They know things will get done when I feel they're important enough.

"I was just passing through to get myself home. Just got done with a case a few days ago and I needed to rest for a bit," I lie.

The siren glances between me and the centaur. "I know we don't really have the jurisdiction, but would you be able to look over the scene and coordinate with the responding agency when they get here? At least this way, *someone* can kick-start this investigation. We can't afford for there to be any more bodies."

"Why not," I say as I stroll over to where the woman lies facedown and squat beside her lifeless body. She's still got some color to her, and when I touch her, I find she's still warm, which means she was likely killed only a few hours ago.

I look back at the siren, hoping she'd be the one to be more aware of her surroundings than her male counterpart, and ask, "Did you guys pass anyone, or anything, on your way into the courtyard?"

Her brows furrow as she takes a moment to think, and then looks at the centaur. "I don't think there was anything that stood out, but I guess I wasn't really paying attention." Of fucking course she wasn't. Assuming makes an ass out of you and me after all. She continues, "One of our tenants in this apartment building told us something weird was going on out here, but wouldn't tell us what, so we just came to check things out."

Quirking my head, I ask, "Wait. Are you guys part of T.I.T.S.?"

Yes, you read that right… T.I.T.S. It's short for Taskforce for the Integration and Tracking of Supernaturals. Whoever named the organization was *not* thinking about what everyone would shorten it down to.

The siren rolls her eyes and huffs out a breath. "I wish people would stop calling it that. It's so fucking childish."

I laugh and shake my head. "Maybe y'all should change the name then."

The centaur joins in my laughter. "I still think it's funny, but clearly not everyone on the force thinks like I do. Especially Maliah here."

Maliah's head whips to where the centaur stands. Her teal eyes take on a metallic shine as she stares him down. "Grow the fuck up, Alastair."

"So testy tonight. Have you not lured someone to their death recently?" Alastair asks with a playful lilt to his voice.

The color of Maliah's eyes intensifies as her cheeks flush a beautiful shade of pink. "That's not fucking funny, and you know it. Especially in the presence of a hunter. While we're mere feet from a dead body."

I shrug my shoulders. "We all do what we have to in order to survive in this world. There isn't a contract out for you, and I know you're a siren, so these marks aren't from you. Nothing to worry about from me."

All color drains from Maliah's face, and her mouth falls open. "That one moment where my glamour slipped wasn't enough for you to tell what I am."

A smirk tips up the corners of my lips. "Sweetheart, I'm a hunter. It's my job to know what—and who—surrounds me at any given time. Plus, I can see through glamour."

Maliah's eyes roll again, and I let out a light laugh before returning my attention to the body before me. I brush the hair from the woman's face, revealing deep gashes across her cheeks and mouth. The four gashes are spaced just far enough apart that I know they were caused by claws.

I run my gaze further down her body, looking for any other wounds the attacker may have inflicted. There's a pool of blood under her midsection, but I can't see the extent of the wound with the way her body is positioned, so I roll her onto her back. On the side that was facing the ground, I see the exact reason why there's so much blood. Her intestines have been ripped apart, and all her remaining organs are now spilling out of her abdomen.

Something feasted on her. And I have a feeling the only reason it stopped was because it was interrupted.

"You guys said this is the third victim, right?" I ask.

Maliah and Alastair sidle up next to me, but the former gags and runs off, retching into the bushes on the opposite side of the courtyard.

"Thank you for taking that elsewhere," I say.

Alastair shifts on his feet. "To answer your question, yes, this is the third victim. They've all been found in courtyards with claw marks across their cheeks and mouths, but this is tame compared to the last one."

"How so?" I ask, thinking I may already know the answer.

"The monster nearly ripped the abdomens of the others in two, and their organs were almost all gone," Alastair explains.

"I think I'm going to be sick again," Maliah whines as she gags.

"Interesting," I muse. Then Maliah retches again. "You ought to get your friend out of here. She clearly doesn't have the stomach for this work. And on your way home—or wherever you're going—could you contact someone so we can get this body out of here? I don't have any contacts nearby."

Alastair hastily steps back. "I'll get in contact with S.I.R.E.N. They should have the other bodies as well. Good luck finding this… thing that's killing these girls."

For fuck's sake, we have a lot of acronyms. S.I.R.E.N.—Supernatural Incident Response and Enforcement Network—is akin to a homicide unit in the human world, but they usually stick to the bigger cities. Given that this city isn't particularly big, I wasn't sure if they'd have a team to cover this area.

"Thanks," I say without looking up from the body.

As they walk away, I mumble to myself, "They sure don't make agents for any of the organizations like they used to—even some of the recent hunters I've met have been lackluster. They're all so sensitive and squeamish nowadays."

I spend a few more minutes looking over the body before I stand to look around the courtyard. It's not big—about the size of a two-bedroom apartment—with a tall tree in the center. I approach the trunk and look up, wondering if the killer could've escaped up it. Since it's likely a supe that's been killing these women, it could've climbed high enough up so it could jump onto one of the roofs. But with the fact I'd been on the roof, I would've seen something because, let's face it, the supe ripped into a woman's abdomen. It had to have left some sort of blood trail when it took off.

Not finding anything suspicious in the tree, I return to the body and look for stray blood droplets in the vicinity. It doesn't take me long to pick up on a minuscule trail—this thing was far cleaner than I expected after what it had done—that leads to the entry of the courtyard. With my head down, following the trail, I run directly into someone. I look up and start to apologize, but immediately stop when I'm met with a face I know all too well, one I'd hoped never to see again. She's still as gorgeous as ever, and it pisses me off.

"Well, well, well. What a pleasant surprise," she says in her sickeningly sweet voice.

Schooling my features to seem indifferent, I say, "Hello, Adrestia. I'd say it's nice to see you too, but that'd be a blatant lie."

She sticks out her bottom lip and attempts to soften her eyes. "You wound me with your words. And by calling me by my full first name. What happened to Addie? I quite miss your calling me that. Actually, I miss a lot about you, Avie."

"You have no right to call me Avie. Not after what you allowed your family to do," I hiss.

She takes a step toward me and drops her glamour, letting her griffin form take over. For whatever reason, she thinks she can intimidate me with how massive she is, but she can't. I've faced off with supes far bigger and scarier than her. I stand my ground, and she growls. The rumble vibrates through my chest, only fueling my intolerance of her.

The timbre of her voice drops several octaves when she speaks again. "You don't know the whole story."

"Nor do I want to. It's in the past; let's leave it there."

Her nostrils flare. "Fine. What are you doing here, Avyanna?"

"I could ask you the same question," I say, gritting my teeth.

Adrestia huffs. "What's with this fucking attitude? Have you not gotten fucked in a while? I can always help you with that."

"You deserve every ounce of attitude I'm giving you right now. I will *never* forgive you, so leave me the fuck alone and—not so kindly—go fuck yourself."

A dry laugh escapes Adrestia's lips as she brings her human glamour back up. "I forgot how dramatic you can be."

"I sure as fuck didn't forget how much of a bitch *you* can be."

"Whatever. Back to the matter at hand. A newer agency by the name of B.I.T.E. hired me to track down whatever has been terrorizing the area, so this is my case. With that being said, your help isn't needed, and you can leave," Adrestia says, flicking her golden hair over her shoulder.

Throwing my hands up, I back away and almost trip over a Jack-o'-lantern in the process. The stupid things litter the entire courtyard. "By all means, be my guest. I'm only here because I happened across the body, and the T.I.T.S. agents asked me to look over things until the responding agency showed up. But you've got this, so I won't bother you with my observations or anything." Then, I turn to leave and flash her both my middle fingers.

Chapter Two

Avyanna

Leave it to me to run into Adrestia in this middle of nowhere city when I've successfully avoided her for decades. I'd hoped never to see her again, to deal with the ache I still have for her. At one point, all those years ago, I thought she actually loved me. But the things she let happen to me aren't something you'd allow the love of your life to go through without intervening. I still haven't forgiven her, nor do I think I ever could.

Now that I'm not working the case, I can focus on finding my girl—as long as she hasn't moved again. She never stays in one spot for long and seems to know when someone has shared her whereabouts with me.

Every time I've gotten close, the home she was staying in has been completely cleaned out, leaving no trace of her behind.

I'm dying to see her in the flesh again, to hopefully touch her and see if she makes me feel the way I hope she does. At this point, I've stared at far too many pictures of the beautiful woman who continuously drifts through my mind and weaves herself into my every dream. It's not enough anymore.

According to my source in the city, the house where Roxanna has supposedly been staying is only about a mile from the crime scene, so I head straight there. On my way there, I try to keep myself hidden as much as possible—going through alleyways and morphing into someone who's not... me. My unusually pale skin and intensely vibrant blue eyes tend to make others feel uneasy. Especially paired with my midnight black hair. I've learned that the best way for me to hide is by blending in.

As I approach the address, I take a look around. All the houses here are stunning, with multiple stories, upscale decor, and immaculate exteriors—par for the course when it comes to my girl.

When I'm sure no one is around to spot me, I drop my glamour and tuck myself into the bushes across the street from her house. I try my best to get comfortable, since I don't plan on leaving until the sun begins to rise. Even then, I don't want to go, but lying in the bushes in a neighborhood like this would draw far more suspicion than I'd like. This is about the only time I wish I were like other shifters—so I could change into an animal.

A light flicks on in a first-floor room, illuminating the space. The first thing that catches my attention is a massive chandelier hanging over a long, sleek dining table with high-backed chairs surrounding it. A massive man—who has to be at least six foot six inches tall—walks across the room into the adjoining kitchen and opens up the fridge. He stands there for a moment before he turns to one of the counters with his back to me. His broad shoulders and muscular build are evident even with the suit jacket he's wearing.

But as I mentioned earlier, appearances can be deceiving. Underneath that glamoured muscular build, he hides a demonic form that stands well over seven feet tall. His soul is marred with thousands of scars, showcasing the lives he's ruined or taken. I make a mental note to keep an eye on him, especially around my girl. She's *mine.* If he lays so much as a finger on her, I will tie him up with blessed chains that will take away any abilities he has, and then I'll break every bone in his body. When he's begging me to save his life, I'll flay his skin layer by layer, making sure he only skirts the edge of death without actually dying until

I'm satisfied. I have zero tolerance for men who can't keep their hands to themselves, given what's happened to me.

Anger has my skin rippling—something that only happens when I'm overly emotional or my power is waning and I need to feed. I take a deep breath and rip my gaze away from the disgusting waste of space. My eyes dart from window to window, trying to find any sign of my girl. Nothing catches my eye, so I wander around to the back of the house. There aren't any lights on back here, but moonlight shines through one window, revealing a luxurious bathroom. In one corner of the room is a massive jacuzzi tub that could fit several people. In the other corner is a beautiful shower with three different-style showerheads, tiled with onyx and emerald green stones. It's beautiful. Perfect for the beautiful woman I seek.

Just as my gaze is about to shift to the next window, light floods the bathroom. My heart rate spikes as the woman I've obsessed over for so long strolls into the room. Her long, silky black hair sways across her pale skin, a stark contrast that gives her a haunting look, but fuck if she isn't a sight for sore eyes.

When she approaches the mirror, I look directly into her eyes without consequence. The photos I've managed to get from my sources don't do them justice whatsoever. Her irises are the most mesmerizing shade of emerald green I've ever seen, and even in her human form, her pupils remain slightly slitted, hinting at what she is. I couldn't imagine not being able to look into those beautiful eyes, even if it means I meet my end.

I allow my eyes to peruse the rest of her body, watching her to see what she does next with rapt attention. My intrigue is piqued when her form begins to change. It starts with her skin, a shimmer slowly changing her pale complexion to a more ashen shade—similar to the stone she can turn others into with a single look. As the shimmering approaches her neck, it reveals small emerald-green scales at her hairline. Then, the shimmer reaches her hair, and strands weave together to form a mass of snakes the same color as the scales at her hairline. Some snakes are longer than others, but they each slither along her back and shoulders as if they're eager to be free.

She stands there for a moment, looking herself over in the mirror, but then she quickly changes back into her human form and whips her head in my direction. Even though I know she can't actually see me nestled in the foliage of her backyard, I still hold my breath. I refuse to scare her off yet; I just got her back.

Her gaze lingers on where I lie for a little longer before she shrugs off her clothes and steps into the glass shower. Steam quickly fills the space, telling me just how hot she likes her showers. She turns her back to one of the showerheads, which has her facing me, and I can't help but wonder if she did that on purpose. Water cascades over her body, making me wish I could embody it so I can caress her naked skin. My mouth waters when she runs her hands through her hair, which causes her back to arch, pushing her tits out further. While they may be small, they're just enough to fill each of my hands. I'll be able to knead them while still having the ability to pinch her nipples and have her writhing beneath my touch.

My pussy throbs, and my skin ripples again, but I refuse to take my eyes off her. She's *not* running away from me again. I'm hoping I don't need to feed again—that my 'hunger' is linked to being in this woman's very naked, very pleasing presence.

I trail my eyes further down her body, admiring her pear-shaped figure. Her hand wanders down her body in the exact path my eyes just took, but she doesn't stop there. She slides her hand down her belly and caresses her thigh. I bite my lip, suppressing a moan before it leaves my lips, all while letting my hand wander between my own thighs. I have to touch myself even though I know I can hardly stimulate my clit through my clothes, but damn if I don't try.

Soap suds trickle down her body, collecting at the apex of her thighs for only a few seconds before she slips her hand in and throws back her head. I swear I can hear her moan from where I sit, but it may be a trick of my mind. All I can think about at this point is how much I'd rather replace her hand with my mouth while her back is up against the wall of that shower, her legs thrown over my shoulders, and her hands tangled in my hair.

Fuck. It's been so long since I've been with someone else. Sadly, I think Adrestia was my last.

The singular thought of the griffin makes me even more horny, and I'm a little perplexed by it. I shouldn't still want her after everything with her family. Apparently, that thought doesn't cross my mind, though, because the next thought that enters my mind is how much better things could be if Adrestia's face was between my thighs while I eat out my girl.

One more flick of my clit has an orgasm crashing through me. It takes everything in me not to scream out my release. It's the best orgasm I've had in who knows how long. It's got me so weak that I have to lie down on the ground for what seems like forever.

When I finally feel like I can function again, I'm disappointed to find that my girl is already done in the shower. I barely catch her walking out the door, wrapped in a fluffy towel. I watch for a moment to see if any of the other lights on this side of the house come on, but I don't see any, so I climb to my feet and rush to the other side of the house.

No lights are on over here either, which has me wondering if she went to bed naked. I groan as my mind goes into overdrive and my clit starts throbbing again. I guess I'll have to dig out my toy collection when I unpack my things. Or maybe I could buy some new ones in preparation for the time I'll have with my girl soon.

The leaves of the bush I'm in rustle, and I leap to my feet, arms poised to fight if needed.

An all too familiar laugh grates on my nerves. "So you've taken to hiding in the bushes to stalk your prey now?"

I roll my eyes and cross my arms over my chest. "What the fuck are you doing here, Adrestia?"

She rakes her eyes down my frame and licks her lips. "I could ask the same thing, Avie."

My nostrils flare. "As I said earlier, you have no right to call me that anymore. How did you even know I was here? It's fucking dark, and your eyesight is nowhere near as good as mine."

Adrestia points her finger at her nose and gives me a sinister smile. "I know your scent. It's something I'll never forget. Just like so many other things about you."

My cheeks pinken. Damn supes and their enhanced sense of smell. And damn her for knowing me at all.

She takes a step toward me and pulls my lip from between my teeth, which I didn't even realize I'd bitten.

"Don't be embarrassed. You know I'm fully capable of taking care of your sexual desires. Just like old times."

For a moment, I consider it—like the idiot she seems to make me. Instead, I force myself to take a step back. Just because my body still wants her doesn't mean she deserves another chance. "Go fuck yourself."

"Damn. Fucking you just sounds so much better, though," she whines.

"Why are you really here, Adrestia?"

She sighs. "I was just passing by the area and scented you."

"You scented my arousal and what? Figured you'd try to weasel your way back into my life by offering to fuck me and essentially 'scratch my itch'? That's low. Even for you," I say, venom dripping from every word.

Adrestia scoffs and crosses her arms. "You can't tell me we weren't good together."

"You're right. I can't. But I can say that you're not worth the pain of having my heart ripped out again. Unless..." I trail off, not really knowing where I was going with that thought.

Her eyebrow rises. "Unless what?"

"Just fuck off, Adrestia. I don't want you anywhere near me. Go work your case," I snap.

"So testy. You must be hungry. I can help you with that, too."

I snarl. "I'm not fucking hungry; I just want you to leave me the fuck alone. Forever, preferably."

She rolls her eyes. "Well, I'll be in the area for a bit. Maybe I'll see you before we inevitably go our separate ways again. Just know I can help with some needs if you'd like me to."

Then she's off, and my pulse is racing. I really need to get fucked. And never to think about her again.

Chapter Three

I swore I felt eyes on me when I dropped my glamour in the bathroom; that's why I put it back up so fast. It absolutely upset my snakes, but my gaze is instantly lethal in my gorgon form. In my human form, it takes at least a little longer to turn someone to stone.

Then, like the idiot I am, I looked out the window for a few minutes, almost as if I was hoping to find someone out there. Being trapped for so long, I've craved attention. The men who guard me will look at my body when I have it on display, which is often, because I love it when people look at me.

Only one has ever had the nerve to touch me, though. His name was Calen, and that night was the best night of my life. My father didn't appreciate my putting his guard in danger, though. He was worried Calen would've looked into my eyes and I would've killed him. So, to punish me for my irresponsibility, he killed Calen and put him on display outside my window for at least a week. Not only did he want me to understand the consequences of my actions, but he wanted the other guards to know what would happen if they ever tried to touch me again.

My father has been gone for several decades now, and the guards who've stuck around still refuse to give in to my advances. It doesn't stop me from giving anyone who's watching a show, though.

After I'm dried off, I climb into bed, not bothering with clothes. I love the feel of silk sheets against my bare skin. But I can't get comfortable because my clit is still throbbing. That orgasm in the shower wasn't nearly enough to satiate me. I toss and turn, trying to ignore it. To my dismay, every time I change positions, it puts more friction on my clit. There really are days when I wish someone were around who'd fuck me.

With a groan, I reach over to my nightstand and pull out my favorite vibrator—good ole pinky. I'm amazed this thing still works with as long as I've had it. Lying on my back, I slip the toy under the covers and position it at my slick entrance. My pussy flutters in anticipation.

Just when I'm about to slide the toy inside me, the shadows in the corner of my room shift, and I stop everything. I lock my eyes on the area, watching to see if someone is in there watching me. The shadows disperse, and out walks one of my guards, Merric, with his eyes cast down.

He's stunning—freakishly tall and super muscular, with blonde hair and intense blue eyes. I've had my eye on him since he started working for my father nearly a century ago. But he'd just started working for my father when Calen was killed, so he's barely paid me any attention over the years. I wonder what he's doing in my room now.

I sit up and allow my comforter to drop to my waist. My breasts are on full display for him to ogle. As expected, his eyes come up to stare at them. Excitement courses through me, and my nipples pebble.

"Do you like what you see?" I ask, shoving the comforter off me and rising to my knees so I'm completely uncovered.

A growl rumbles in his chest. "As a matter of fact, I do. I've always been warned not to touch you, but there's no one else here, so how would they know if I took a quick taste?"

I lick my lips and crawl to the edge of the bed near him. "I'll give you more than just a taste if that's what you want."

He lifts me into his arms, and I wrap my legs around his waist, his hard length rubbing against my clit. Our mouths collide in a messy kiss, but he's pulling away all too fast when he lays me down on the bed. As he stands, his gaze locks between my splayed legs, and my pussy flutters, showing off for him.

"You're already so wet," he says, voice husky. Then he spots my vibrator lying next to me and raises a brow. "Did I interrupt something?"

"I hadn't quite started yet, so you came at the perfect time."

A smile spreads across his face as he drops to his knees. "Glad I can be of service."

I wiggle my hips in anticipation, and he grabs them, yanking my ass to the edge. Then his tongue is gliding through my wetness. I've never done this before, and fuck does it feel good. My hips try to buck, but he keeps a tight grip on me. He licks me like he's a man starved and has done this a million times—which he probably has. I can't stop the whimpers and moans that slip past my lips.

Shadows snake up my body and cover my mouth. "Quiet, pretty little curse. Just because we're all alone doesn't mean I want anyone nearby to hear you either."

I do my best to stay quiet, but when he continues his pursuit, he slips one thick finger into me and then another, and I can't stop the screams. His shadows at my mouth thicken to quiet my screams, nearly suffocating me. The mix of his fingers and tongue is an exquisite feeling, taking me to heights my vibrator never could before. I won't last long like this.

Lifting his head from me, he says, "That's it. Come on my fingers and tongue. I want you soaked when I fuck your cunt."

His tongue returns to my pussy, and he shoves it into me. It seems to elongate, reaching high up to the spot I can't even seem to reach with my toy most of the time. He strokes it quickly, moving his fingers in time with it, and my toes curl.

I'm so fucking close.

My screams even out—still barely contained by the shadows over my mouth—so he shifts his hand, allowing his thumb to play with my clit. That's all it takes for me to come undone. My back bows off the bed as my body convulses, wave after wave of pleasure rippling through me. His strokes slow as I come down from my high, and he pulls his tongue from my pussy to lap at my arousal.

When he stands, he licks his lips with his eyes still lingering on my pussy. "You taste so good—like the most succulent forbidden fruit I've ever bitten into. I can't wait to sink my cock into your tight cunt and fill you with my cum while you squirm beneath me."

My eyes widen, and I'm about to object when a feminine voice growls, "Over my dead body will that *ever* fucking happen."

I shoot up in bed and dart my eyes around to look for the source. A woman steps out of the shadows where Merric had been watching me, skin literally rippling, changing shades before me. And her eyes... They're going back and forth between glacial blue and pure black. I've never seen anything like it before.

Her gaze is fixed on Merric, whose eyes widen as he takes a step away from my bed. I watch, terror rising, while Merric takes on his demon form. He grows over a foot taller than his already massive frame, stretching out the muscle and fat of his body, making him look scrawny. At the same time, his skin turns ashen, and shadows curl around his limbs like he's preparing to fight.

He clenches his hands, and an unfamiliar, deep, raspy voice leaves him, reverberating through my bedroom. "Who the fuck are you?"

A wicked smile crosses the woman's lips. "Who I am doesn't matter. I have a feeling you know the answer to that question, though. You demons don't spook easily."

"What do you want, hunter?" Merric asks.

Her lip curls as she takes a step toward him. "To relieve you of your fucking head."

Merric laughs, which seems to make the woman even more furious. "Get in line. There are millions on this Earth who would like my head served to them on a platter because of something or another that I've done. You tend to piss a lot of people off when you've been alive as long as I have," he says, rolling his eyes. "I must say, I don't think I've ever pissed a hunter off before. How did I manage that?"

"First off, you touched what was not yours to touch. Then—" she hisses before Merric barks out another laugh.

"Not mine to touch? I'll do whatever I please with her. She walks around this house flaunting her body, begging to be fucked. We all know it's exactly what she wants, but everyone else is too chickenshit to do it themselves. Even if she doesn't, all I have to do is avoid her gaze, so she doesn't turn me to stone. A blindfold would easily do the trick. Not like there's been anyone around to stop me ever since her father died," he says in a relaxed voice that makes my stomach turn.

Fury washes through me, boiling my blood until fire is rushing through my veins. I shoot to my feet, dropping my human glamour to let my snakes free, and bring myself face-to-face with Merric. He looks away from me, but I reach up and dig my nails into his cheeks, forcing him to look at me. His eyes slam shut, and I let out a menacing laugh.

"You're fucking pathetic. Why don't you open your eyes and face me like the man you seem to think you are?" I hiss along with my snakes.

He rips his face away from me, and dark, sticky blood streams from the spots where my nails dug into his skin. "You're fucking crazy if you think I'd do that, especially while you're in your gorgon form."

The woman appears before Merric in the blink of an eye. She somehow manages to grow a couple of feet taller, making her eye level with him, and wraps her hand around his throat. "You were so eager to tell me you would take her however you pleased, even if it were against her will. Yet you don't have the decency to *look* at her when she is speaking to you. Even if it isn't in the eyes, she deserves your entire fucking attention. You're a fucking coward and a disgusting waste of space."

"I'm not risking turning to stone for a fucking whore!" he yells, shadows tracking up his neck to grab at the woman's hand on his throat.

My hands shake, and the snakes on my head hiss as they snap at Merric. When I speak, I don't recognize my voice. "A whore? Because I want attention, which I've been deprived of for my entire *life*, because of what I am? I *let* you touch me; I didn't beg you to. There's a big fucking difference. You were the one who showed up in my bedroom without an invitation. And then, when I was about to let you fuck me, you proceeded to tell me you'd fill me with your cum without making sure I was okay with it. I am not here for you to do with as you please, even though you seem to think that's the case. I never want to see you again, Merric. You're dismissed."

The woman's hand tightens around his throat. Her black eyes gleam with excitement, and the corner of her lips tips up into a taunting, dangerous smile. "You and I are about to have a lot of fun, *Merric*. Letting you look into her eyes would be a mercy too nice for you, especially after what you tried to do to her. I'm going to enjoy torturing you."

My attention shifts to the woman, and I quirk my head. "Who the hell are you?"

"I'm a monster hunter—part of the organization D .A.M.N.E.D," she says, features softening.

"Oh," I whisper, my eyes widening. "Did he do something to warrant a hunter coming after him?" She shakes her head, her black wavy hair swaying back and forth across her back, and my brows furrow. "What are you doing here then?"

She sighs and clenches her jaw. "I'm here to make sure I don't lose you again, Roxanna."

I take a step back from her and Merric. "Again? What's that supposed to mean?"

"Don't ask questions you don't want the answers to," she says as if that would make sense to me.

My heartbeat goes wild, and I ball my hands into fists, prepared to attack if it comes down to it. "I absolutely want to know what the fuck you mean by that!"

"Just catching sight of you *once* several decades ago, I knew you were different. You make me feel different, and I need to know why, so I've been tracking you ever since you got away from me all those years ago," she whispers.

I let her words settle in. "You're here because of some weird infatuation with me?"

A mirthless laugh leaves her lips. "My Little Relic, this is far more than an infatuation; it's a full-blown obsession, and I'm not letting you get away again."

I take a step toward the door, and her head whips in my direction. When our eyes meet, I hold my breath.

I'm in my gorgon form.

I'm going to turn her to stone, kill her—which I oddly want to avoid—so I avert my gaze and run.

Chapter Four

Avyanna

When our eyes meet, I'm prepared to turn to stone, grateful for the little bit I was able to get. As she races from the room, I allow my eyes to drift shut, so I can savor the image of her being so close, yet still too far to touch.

But when nothing happens, my eyes fly open to look in the mirror. Merric uses my distraction to attempt an escape, which only serves to irritate me. He raises his fists to swing at my face, but I slam his back against the wall, knocking the wind out of him. The demon attempts to hit me again, and I squeeze his throat a little tighter, digging my nails into his flesh. As much as I want to torture the bastard, finding—and keeping—the gorgon is more important to me, so I rip out his windpipe. His body slides down the wall, and I watch as he drops to the floor, sticky, acrid blood pouring from the gaping hole in his throat.

Dropping the piece of flesh beside him, I walk over to the bed, grab the comforter, and try to clean my hand off as much as I can. I'm able to get the majority of it off before an intense blue light fills the room. I don't even bother turning around because I know exactly who it is, and I don't have time for his shit right now.

"Why does it not surprise me that this is your doing, hunter?" a familiar voice says behind me.

"Because this is what I do? I hunt down pieces of trash that don't deserve to live. He was a shitty excuse for a fucking bodyguard who was about to force himself onto a woman," I growl. "Not to mention, that woman is *mine*. No one can touch what's mine without fucking consequences."

The man gives a gruff laugh. "All of you shifters are so possessive and grumpy. You should ease up a little, Anna."

I drop the comforter and turn to face the demon most refer to as 'The Retriever'. But I knew Alaric before he was given that title. "I'm not just any shifter, which is something you should know very well by now, seeing as we've known each other for centuries. This woman—who is currently getting farther and farther from me as we speak—has occupied every inch of my mind since I saw her several *decades* ago. No one has ever made me feel the way she does, just from one glance. She's gotten away from me far too many times, and I won't stop my pursuit until I have her in my clutches once and for all."

Alaric shakes his head. "I pity anyone who gets in your way—until you get bored with her, at least. It's bound to happen at some point; it's what happened with Adrestia. You were obsessed with her until you weren't. I swear you were looking for a reason to get rid of her, and her family gave you the perfect out."

Anger surges, and I'm seeing red as I step toward the demon. "You'd better watch what you're saying, otherwise the demons may have to find themselves a new 'Retriever'. It'd be a shame after all the years you've been with them."

Alaric rolls his eyes. "I'm shaking in my boots, Anna. You don't scare me."

"Well, let's just get one thing straight then. Adrestia's family auctioning me off to sex traffickers was not an excuse to be rid of her! What sealed her fate was the fact that she didn't even try to help me when she found out what her family had done."

His eyebrow raises as he stares me down. "You really think she just stood by and let those men do as they pleased with you without interfering? How the hell do you think you were able to get out? You're an extremely strong and smart woman, but I highly doubt you'd be able to get out of a situation like that without a little bit of help—just saying. Then, when you got out, she tried to give you some space before she approached you, but you disappeared before she had a chance, and she didn't want to chase after you. I can't really blame her for that."

I take a deep breath and roll my eyes. "Whatever. I don't have time to listen to you ramble about shit that doesn't matter anymore."

He scoffs. "Well, go on then. I'll take care of our friend here."

"Goodbye, Alaric," I say as I turn to leave.

"Enjoy your chase, Anna."

I follow the scent of Roxanna's fear down the hall to another bedroom very similar to hers. Several drawers on the dresser hang open, and a door on the opposite wall is wide open. I walk over to it and peer inside, only to find a closet full of outdated shirts and pants that I doubt my girl would ever wear. The amount of clothing scattered on the floor in this otherwise well-kept space makes me think I'm correct in that assumption. She went through nearly half the closet before finding something she was willing to wear. Maybe I've underestimated her fear.

Moonlight streams through another open doorway around the corner, which leads to a lavish bathroom. This one differs entirely from the one I saw my girl in earlier. Every surface of this bathroom is pure white, while the fixtures—the sinks, tub, and showerheads to be exact—are all made of real gold. It's such an incredible sight, and if I weren't already in a rush, I'd love to bask in its beauty.

Across the room from me, curtains flutter, revealing a wide-open window. My first thought is that my girl has made a run for it by jumping out this damn window, and I'm going to have to chase her down. Excitement courses through me—I love a good hunt, and that's what this is turning out to be.

Peering out, I watch as Roxanna runs down the street, her silky hair glinting in the moonlight. Watching her, I notice that her hair has a greenish tint to it, linking even further to her gorgon form. I let her run until she's nearly out of my sight. Then, I propel myself out the window, landing gracefully on my feet, and take off at a full run. Even with my speed, my footfalls are silent—something that took me decades to master. I don't want to alert her to my presence until she's in my arms. She likely thinks I'm dead, and I'm really amazed I'm not, but I'm about to turn her whole world upside down.

It takes me less than a minute to catch up to her. When I do, I wrap my arms around her and take her down to the ground. "You can't escape from me that easily, my little relic."

She lets out a shriek, and I laugh as we collide with the grass.

Being the feisty woman she is, she struggles against me until I ease my hold. When her eyes land on me, her mouth falls open. "I-I didn't turn you to stone. How? I was in my gorgon form."

"Your guess is as good as mine, but I'm here now and I'm going to make the best of it," I say with a smirk, rolling her so she's on her back and I'm wedged between her thighs. Putting all my weight on my forearms, which are on either side of her head, I ask, "Why did you run?"

Her gaze drifts to the tree beside us. "I don't know. Part of me was scared Merric would escape your hold and come after me when you turned to stone—that he'd finish what he started."

A growl rumbles in my chest. "I would never have let that happen."

She purses her lips. "How could you have stopped him if you'd turned to stone?"

I grab her chin and turn her face to look at me. This time, she doesn't fight. She looks at me with those mesmerizing eyes, full of tears that have yet to spill. They're even more vibrant green than they'd been at the house, and I can't imagine never being able to look into them again.

"Well, it didn't happen, and I'll make sure nothing like that happens ever again," I whisper.

A tear streaks down her cheek, and she sniffles. "You don't even know me."

"I know there's something different about you."

"What if it's something you don't like?"

I shake my head. "I don't think there could be a single thing about you I won't like. You're more likely to find things about me you don't like."

"Like what?"

I give her a sly smirk. "You're going to have to stick around and find out for yourself. I'm not letting you run off yet. Well, unless you like being chased."

Her cheeks flush a beautiful shade of red. "I wouldn't know. I've kind of been locked inside houses for my entire life and haven't tried to run away from someone until now."

"Well, we'll have to do some... research at some point."

"What's that supposed to mean?" she asks hesitantly.

I run my tongue piercing over my lip. "We're going to have so much fun, pretty girl. Just you wait."

She stares at me with her brows drawn together, and I laugh because she has no idea what I have in store for her. After a moment, I get to my feet and hold out a hand to her. One of her eyebrows raises as she takes it.

I pull her to her feet and swoop her up into my arms bridal style. "You're coming home with me, and I won't be letting you go anytime soon."

Her eyes widen, and her breathing picks up as she tries to shove away from me. All I do is laugh because I know her attempts are futile.

"If all you intend to do is lock me up, you may as well put me down now. I will *not* go from one prison to another!" she shrieks.

My steps falter. "Who said I was going to lock you up?"

Her brows draw together again. "You just said you weren't going to be 'letting me go anytime soon'."

A harsh laugh escapes me, and I continue walking. "I didn't mean that in the literal sense. You're your own person, so you can do whatever it is you please, but I won't let you leave *me*. You're *mine* from this day forward. Hell, you've been mine since the first time I saw you."

Chapter Five

ADRESTIA

Walking away from Avie this evening was so fucking hard. I could smell her arousal, and my tail tried to get away from me a time or two. It wanted to sneak between her thighs and tell me just how wet she was. Hell, if she'd let me, I would've taken her right there, on the ground in front of the house she was watching. She never shied away from public sex; she loves to watch and to be watched.

Fuck. Now I'm hot and bothered again just thinking about her and her damn arousal.

When I showed up at the crime scene and found her there this evening, I was shocked. Per usual, all-black gear covered nearly every inch of her pale skin—which

I confirmed this evening is still as soft as the last time I touched it. Then, after she ran into me, her beautiful, icy blue eyes looked up at me through those thick lashes of hers, and my heart flipped-flopped for the first time in far too many years.

It's been longer than I'd like to admit since I saw her last, and I wish we could go back to the way things were before my family fucked everything up. Her absence has left a gaping hole in my heart that I tried to remedy by slapping a band-aid over it. Seeing her today ripped the motherfucker off, and I'm hurting all over again. I've missed my little mimic so fucking much.

I'm glad to see that she's as feisty as ever, though. She's done well for herself, even with everything my family did. Nearly everyone in the supernatural community knows who she is—she's the best hunter there is, after all—and she's always the first person everyone recommends when a supe needs to be eradicated. I'm proud of her, though I doubt she'll believe me if I get a chance to tell her.

Seeing her has made me realize how badly I need her back in my life, but I know I'll have to prove myself again. I just don't know if that'll be enough for her.

She's always been skeptical of the world, rightfully so with everything she's been through in her life. Even with that, she let me in—let me love her and take care of her—but my family completely fucked that up for me.

When they first heard that I was dating a 'skinwalker', they threw a fit. I brushed them off for a while, but then they tried to make me choose between them and her. According to them, she wasn't suitable for me, not good enough because of what she was and the work she did.

In their defense, people of her kind are rare, so little is known about them, but many consider them to be dangerous. Most supes think her kind are monsters who must be eradicated, that they feast on others because they can, not because they need to. However, being with Avie, I knew that wasn't true.

I tried to counter my family's accusations and explain that she was a good person deep down, even though she'd been through a lot of shit. They wanted no part in it, insisting that my relationship with a 'skinwalker' looked bad on the family, and I needed to end it.

That's the shitty thing about my family. They've always been about what's best for them as a whole, regardless of how it affects the people involved. As griffins, we're expected to stay loyal to our family no matter the situation. The expectation was for me to choose my family.

But they've never deserved my loyalty or thought about the consequences of their actions if things didn't go in their favor, so I chose my little mimic without thought.

Unfortunately, before I had the chance to tell her, my family abducted her from the apartment we shared and sold her off to the highest bidder—a sex trafficking ring. I was livid with them and went behind their backs to do everything in my power to free her.

Once she was out, I killed those she hadn't been able to during her escape. She needed space, which I was more than happy to give her for a while. But when I returned from tracking down the rest of the ring, she was gone, and I didn't have it in me to look for her again.

After everything was said and done, I disowned my family and left the apartment I shared with Avyanna. My family has tried to contact me several times over the years, but they've never apologized for what they've done. To this day, the only reply I've sent them is 'go fuck yourselves'.

I spent several years wandering around the world, hoping I'd run into Avie, to no avail. That's when I met Bella. I was one of the first recruits for Belladonna's Investigations, Tracking, and Elimination (B.I.T.E.). Over the years, she's become one of my closest friends. She's always seen my potential and has pushed me to become the best I can be.

Since I've joined B.I.T.E., Bella and I have worked to expand the organization throughout the United States, and I've moved around the country several times to help wherever I'm needed. Recently, my focus has been on training new recruits while I set up new bases for our agents to work from. The outpost we're setting up in this city is brand new, so I've come to make sure it's a suitable location for us. I also want to see what kind of supes are in the area.

The next step in this process was for Bella to send out some potential agents, but that's been put on hold with this thing killing women. While you might think that already having cases here would be beneficial for training agents, this case has quickly proven how dangerous our target is. I refuse to risk the lives of brand-new agents until I know more about this thing.

Needless to say, this case is all mine to work on, and I really need to fucking focus before things get worse. This monster has already managed to kill three women, and I need to stop it before it adds another to its body count.

Now that I've run into Avie again, things are a little more difficult. I feel like I have to make everything up to her and explain exactly what happened. I don't want to let her go again. But I guess that's not really my choice to make at this point. No matter what the outcome is, I just want her to be happy.

I shake my head, trying to get my thoughts away from my past as I stroll into a large expanse of trees down the street. Since I move frequently, I refuse to buy a car, so I take to the skies when I have a long distance to go. Or when I just want to get to my destination faster.

The moment I'm certain no one can see me, I drop my glamour and let my wings unfurl. I'm careful not to let them slam into the trees, but it feels good to let them free after having them restricted for several days in a row. Then, I dig my talons on my front feet into the dirt while my paws on my back feet flex. The first time I took on my human form, I hated how small my feet felt beneath me, how cramped my talons felt in my hands. As most of us supes would say, we're more comfortable in our true form.

Once I've stretched everything out, I push off the ground and flap my wings a few times to propel myself into the air. I soar up into the clouds, where I know I'll be more hidden, and glide across the city toward my building. The wind beneath me cools my all-too-hot skin from my encounter with Avyanna. She always had a way of making me lose myself in her presence; it appears now is no different.

As I fly, I glance down at the city below me, making sure nothing seems out of sorts. As much as I'd like to say I haven't spotted anything before, I have. This city is a mess, and there've been at least a dozen murders since I arrived. Not many have been by the hand of a supe thus far, but people are getting away with too much. The human police can't keep up, and there aren't enough supe agencies here to help them control those who step out of line.

It's why Bella and I wanted to bring B.I.T.E. here. We want to help these people. I just kind of wish I had some help. I'm only one person, and there's a lot of shit to take care of here. But I don't dare tell Bella because she'll put the staff in more danger than it's worth. Once I can get rid of whatever is going after these girls, Bella can bring others in, and I'll be able to focus on my little mimic more. Until then, I'll have to take things as they come.

This whole ordeal is going to be a test of my patience. If I'm not careful, I risk creating problems that could be detrimental to the people living in this city. That's not something I can afford to let happen. Not only will Bella have my ass for making the agency look bad, but I could chase off Avyanna and ruin any chance I have with her before I even get it.

Taking all of that into consideration, I turn my attention to scanning the streets below. I realize that was a stupid idea when I collide with something and nearly tumble to the ground. A pair of arms wrap around me, and I'm no longer falling, which only serves to freak me out more. I haven't met another flying supe in the area, and I have no clue what the fuck is happening right now.

"You alright down there? I won't be able to hold you like this forever. You're much larger than I am, and my arms are already starting to get pretty tired," a sweet voice says.

My eyes snap open, and I'm met with an intense, stormy grey gaze, reminding me of the clouds on a rainy day. Platinum blonde hair swishes across her gaze, breaking my concentration. My gaze shifts higher to her hairline, where I'm shocked to find feathers almost the same color as her hair peaking out between the strands of her mostly braided hair.

That's when I notice her wings flapping, even though her arms are around me. "How are you still flying? Are your arms not attached to your wings?"

Her eyebrow raises with a slight smirk playing at the corner of her lips. "Those are the questions you have for me?"

"I, uh, I have a lot more, but those are two at the forefront of my mind right now."

She laughs, a beautiful sound I'd like to hear more of. "Interesting. Well, as much as I'd like to keep talking with your body up against mine like this, I need to know if you're able to fly because if you can't, we're going to have to find somewhere to land. I won't be able to carry you for much longer."

"I'm fairly certain I can fly. You just scared me. And your eyes... They're hypnotizing," I say, making a fool of myself.

She gives me a sad smile and loosens her grip on me. I call forth my wings to make sure they catch me when I begin to fall. I'm thankful they work fine, but part of me wishes they didn't because I want to stay in her arms.

Her voice pulls me from my thoughts. "You okay?"

With a small smile of my own, I nod. "Thank you. Would you like to come to my place for a drink... or two? As a thank you for catching me when I so rudely ran into you."

She bites her lip and doesn't answer for a moment, letting the suspense build. "I would love that, actually."

It doesn't take us long to get to my place. When we both land on my patio, more questions spring to mind. I knew she wasn't joking when she said I'm much larger than she is, but standing next to each other is a whole other story—especially while I'm in my griffin form.

Before bombarding her with questions, I summon my human form, keeping my eyes on her as my body compacts itself and I shrink a few inches. But even at this height, I'm several inches taller than she is in her harpy form. "How the hell did you wrap your arms around me and keep me from falling?"

Her wings fold around her. "Just because I'm small doesn't mean I'm not strong."

"That's not at all what I'm insinuating. How did you get your arms around me when I'm so much bigger than you, even in my human form?"

"Do the logistics really matter?" she asks.

"I suppose not, but I do want to thank you again."

She unfolds her wings from around herself, and lightning flashes all over her body, slowly putting her human form in place. After it's all done, she's a couple of inches shorter, and I admire just how muscular she is. As we stand there staring at each other, I trail my eyes down her body and lick my lips. She's delicious in all the best ways—just what I need to get my mind off my little mimic for a little bit.

Chapter Six

Vaelyn

I watch in fascination as the griffin magically un-locks the balcony doors to her penthouse. It's something I've never seen done before, but it's not like I've ever spent long in one place. In the few seconds it takes her to unlock the door, I marvel at the way her shirt clings to her muscular back, showing off every line, indent, and dimple the muscles create. It takes everything in me to keep from tracing the deep groove of her spine down to her luscious ass.

Once the door is unlocked, she pulls it open and ges-tures for me to enter. I whisper a quick thanks before strolling in, eyes widening as I take in the space. Her living room is massive with a vaulted ceiling—which makes sense with the size of her griffin form and how fucking tall she is in general—and decorated to the nines. Being the airborne creature she naturally is, every wall facing the outside of the building is made of floor-to-ceiling windows. I have to say, if I settled down anywhere, this would be exactly what I'd want.

The griffin walks past me, straight into the open-concept kitchen. "What can I get you to drink?"

"Water would be great for now. Thanks," I say, still admiring her penthouse.

She pulls two glasses from the cupboard, fills them, and approaches me, handing me the water I requested. "Thanks again for catching me. I'm still impressed you managed that, considering my size. But, where are my manners?" she says, scoffing at herself. Then, she holds out her hand to me. "My name is Adrestia."

I raise an eyebrow and reach out to shake her hand. "I'm Vaelyn. It's a pleasure to meet you."

A smile spreads across her lips as she releases my hand. "I'm not sure I've ever heard that name, but it's beautiful."

I let out a nervous laugh. "Well, my parents thought they were being funny when they chose my name. Many cultures speak of the 'vale' where their dead go, but according to lore, it's rumored that a harpy's 'victims' never truly enter that 'vale'."

She holds back a laugh. "I'm glad to hear my parents weren't the only ones who named their child with the meaning of the name in mind. My parents thought it was a good idea to name me after the Greek goddess of retribution and balance because I'm a griffin. It's ironic how disloyal I am to them. They've done some really fucked up shit, and they only care about themselves."

"I'm sorry. I can understand that, though. We harpies rarely stray far from our families—whether they be of our blood or those we choose. I never felt like I belonged, and my family never did anything to help alleviate that feeling. If anything, I feel like they pushed me out, so I haven't settled down since the moment I could leave the nest."

Adrestia takes a sip of her water. "I wish I could've been that brave the first moment I realized it was a problem."

"Being by myself hasn't been easy, but I'm relatively glad I did it."

"I can only imagine. When I finally left my family, it felt freeing, but being without a companion even feels… lonely," she says, biting her lip as her eyes drift to the floor. She takes a deep breath and looks back at me. "Enough about that. Are you hungry? I could find us something to eat if you are."

Playing with my venom tongue piercings, I swipe my tongue over my bottom lip. Adrestia's honey-colored eyes darken as she watches me, giving away how my actions are affecting her. I roll my bottom lip between my teeth and set my glass down on the nearby coffee table. She watches me intently as I approach her.

"I can think of something right here that'll satisfy a craving I have," I whisper.

Her lips tip up into a sinful smirk. "Is that so?"

"You can't tell me you haven't been thinking the same thing. I saw the way you looked at me on the balcony when I pulled on my human glamour."

She takes a step toward me, eyes hooded. "I'm going to enjoy putting that pretty mouth to work since you like to run it so damn much."

I roll my tongue piercings over my lip, making her wait for my response. "Why don't you make me?"

She groans. "You're a brat, too. Whose good graces am I in today?"

"You say that now. Just wait, because I'll make you work for it," I snark.

"That makes it all the more fun," she says as she grabs me by the throat and pushes me toward the couch.

When my knees hit the edge, it jostles my clit piercing, and I whimper. It's been a while since I've let someone touch me. That's just what happens when you move around so damn much; you don't get to form connections. And I hate hook-ups so damn much.

Something just feels different with Adrestia, though. I love the feel of her against me, the way she's already making me feel after such a short time. There's something in me that's screaming for me to touch her and to let her touch me. If she doesn't touch me, I feel like I'm going to combust. I've never *needed* someone as much as I need her at this very moment.

"Are you just going to stand there and hold me by the throat? Or are you going to actually do something?" I ask, voice husky.

"That mouth is going to get you into trouble. But I'm going to guess you like to be punished," she says, and my clit throbs.

I roll my tongue piercings over my lip again. "Pain only makes the pleasure sweeter, if you ask me. The more, the better."

She groans and then crashes her lips to mine in a messy kiss. I part my lips just in time for her tongue to tangle with mine. Her hand moves from my throat to the nape of my neck, pulling me flush against her. My hands come to rest on her hips and slip under her shirt. She sharply inhales when my cool hands meet her warm skin. Once my hands warm up, I slide them up toward her breasts. I'm pleased to find she's not wearing a bra, allowing me easy access. My small hands cup her breasts, and my fingers find her nipples with ease. I trace around them to start with, but when I pinch the hardened peaks, I nearly moan. They're pierced. I'm an absolute sucker for a woman with nipple piercings. Her kissing pauses when I squeeze her nipples harder, and she moans into my mouth, so I take the opportunity to bite her lip.

A dark chuckle rumbles from her chest, and in the next moment, her hands are under my ass, lifting me. "You're going to pay for that, little one."

I wrap my legs around her waist, at least the best as I can, and my arms snake around her neck. In the most playful tone I can muster, I say, "I'm so scared."

"Oh, you should be," she says as she carries me further into the penthouse.

Enjoying the teasing, I lean in and pepper her neck with kisses. My clit is now full on pulsing with each step she takes, and I'm fighting not to rock my hips—to increase the delicious friction my body craves.

I didn't think the penthouse was that big, but it feels like it takes forever to get to our destination. As soon as we step out of the hallway and through the doorway into another room, I look around. Again, my eyes widen as I take in my surroundings.

While I still think her living room is stunning, her bedroom is exquisite. There's an entire wall of windows with beautifully detailed burgundy curtains pulled open, revealing the city below. In the distance, the mountains that my heart longs for line the skyline, each peak topped in snow that I hope one day to see again. At the center of the room is a massive four-poster bed made of deep mahogany wood. Gauzy curtains drape over the sides, just as you hear about in stories, and the bedding, in the same burgundy color as the curtains, is laid out perfectly, as if the bed was made right before we arrived. Whoever put this room together took the time to make sure that each component complements the others.

"This is… I don't even have words for it," I whisper.

Adrestia chuckles and throws me down on the bed. "Just wait until you see what it's hiding. It's spectacular. However, before we get started satisfying this craving you have, let's discuss limits and establish a safe word."

I roll my tongue piercings behind my teeth and purse my lips. "Nothing is off the table with me. I haven't found anything I couldn't handle thus far in my sexual escapades. So, needless to say, I don't need a safe word."

"That's great that you haven't found any limits, but I'm not risking anything. Safe word. Now."

"Ooh. So feisty. I like it," I tease, waggling my brows.

Her nostrils flare, and she clenches her teeth. "I mean it, Vaelyn. Give me a safe word; otherwise, we're not doing this."

I roll my eyes and oblige. "Fine. Bananas."

In a sing-song voice, she says, "It's bananas, B-A-N-A-N-A-S?"

"Did you seriously just quote 'Hollaback Girl' by Gwen Stefani?"

A mischievous glint appeared in her eyes. "What if I did?"

I let out a loud laugh. "That's the funniest thing I've ever heard."

"I'm glad I can make you laugh. Now it's time to make you come."

Just the thought of her touching me has wetness pooling between my thighs. "What are you waiting for?"

She reaches for my pants and plays with the waistband. "It's pretty hard to make you come when you're still fully clothed."

I shrug. "It can still be done."

Her hands stop their teasing movements, and I almost whimper. She smirks. "My plans include every single article of clothing coming off you. From here on out, every time you backtalk, you'll be getting a spanking."

If she weren't standing between my spread legs, I would rub them together to relieve some of the pressure on my clit. "That doesn't sound like much of a punishment. I love a good spanking."

"We'll see how much you like them when I'm the one giving them," she says as she finally unbuttons my pants and pulls them off. Then she runs her hands up my bare legs. Her featherlight touch has goose bumps rising and shivers coursing through my body. "Sensitive, are we?"

"A little."

With a playful smile, she yanks my underwear off. "Sit up."

"Yes, ma'am," I say playfully.

To her displeasure, I take my time doing as she says. With each stretch and slow movement, I watch her eyes grow darker. "You're asking for a spanking."

I roll over onto my belly and bring my knees below me so my ass is up in the air. She doesn't take the bait, and I'm slightly disappointed. When I rise onto my knees, though, she takes me by surprise and yanks my shirt over my head. I'm not wearing a bra either, so she has easy access to my breasts. She palms them with her large hands, and I moan, leaning back into her chest.

"Now that you're fully naked, the fun can begin," she whispers in my ear. Then she pinches my nipples and lightly bites my shoulder before shoving me back onto my belly. I catch myself just before my face makes contact with the bedding, but she grips my hips and pulls my ass up in the air, so my face ends up buried after all. Adrestia runs one hand over my bare ass, and the other holds onto my hip, trying to keep me from moving.

I wiggle impatiently, and she rewards me with the smack on my ass I've been dying for. A whimper leaves me only to be swallowed up by the bed.

But the smack wasn't hard enough.

I want more.

She rubs my tingling skin for a moment before she hits me harder. It's still not enough.

"Harder," I say, turning my head so she can hear me.

She returns to rubbing my ass. "Patience, little one. I'm just getting started."

"Patience is *not* a word in my vocabulary, lioness."

"Then you're going to have to learn it. Or I can teach it to you," she says, smacking my ass again. This time it's a little harder.

I hiss at the contact—a slight sting developing where she hit me—which quickly turns to a moan. "What is it that the humans say? You can't teach an old dog new tricks? Give me everything you've got. I want it *harder*."

"Do I have a masochist on my hands? I'm already hitting you pretty hard."

Her hand comes down again, harder on my ass, and I moan. "I would've thought you'd picked that up a little earlier when I told you the more pain, the better."

She doesn't rub my skin again before her hand makes contact, and I'm sharply inhaling. "I've told you what will happen if you backtalk."

"And I've told you that spankings are not a good form of punishment for me. I'll gladly let you smack my ass until I'm so sore I can't sit for days."

As she rubs my ass, she hums. "Then maybe I need to find something you don't like, but will tolerate."

"Good luck. I haven't found anything so far."

She smacks me harder than before, and I rock forward to the best of my ability before she's pulling me right back to her again. "Roll onto your back and lie in the middle of the bed. I'll be right back."

When her hand leaves my hip, I collapse on my belly. My pussy is throbbing so hard that I'm afraid that if I put any pressure on my clit, I'm going to come. It's something I'd usually be okay with, but I don't want to disappoint Adrestia.

That's a first.

After a few deep breaths, my pussy calms, and I'm able to shift myself to the middle of the bed, where she told me to lie. I'm there for several minutes, waiting for her to return. Anticipation builds as I wait longer and longer.

When she finally comes back into the room, I move to sit up, but she's already there, standing over me. She grips my throat and growls, "Stay lying down like a good girl, and I might give you what you so desperately want."

I raise an eyebrow at her. "Might?"

Her eyes never leave mine as she moves her hand from my throat to my wrist. She ties the rope around it and pulls the other end through a hoop in the bedpost, stretching my arm out until I'm barely able to move it before she ties it off. "You've talked back to me. Now I get to decide if you've been punished enough."

"By using bondage? Kinky—literally. I like it."

She tsks at me, her gaze following her hand as she skims her fingers down my arm and across my chest, where she stops to play with my nipple for a moment before continuing down my leg. When she reaches my ankle, I'm practically squirming off the bed, dying for her to touch me. She knows how it's affecting me, too, because when she ties up my ankle, a devious smile graces her lips. Once she's satisfied with that knot, she walks around the bed to tie up my other arm and leg.

With each knot, my chest grows heavier and heavier. I love being tied up by my partners, but I absolutely hate not having an out. My first instinct is always to flee when things go awry, but being completely tied up doesn't give me the ability to do that. Right now, I'm entirely at Adrestia's mercy, and that scares the absolute fuck out of me. Although I don't hate it, for some reason.

My heart feels like it's going to beat out of my chest when she ties the last knot. Her fingers move down my arm and start to pass by my shoulder, but she brings them back to my neck, where she lightly presses two fingers into my pulse point. "Is that from excitement or fear?" she asks in a sultry voice. "I bet you're soaked either way."

"Why don't you find out for yourself?" I tease, knowing she's right. Fear makes me so wet, and I've never understood why.

Her hand leaves my neck and then comes down on my exposed pussy, smacking it hard. I sharply inhale on impact, but a moan quickly follows. She doesn't move her hand, though. Instead, she spreads me open and moves to pinch my clit, but stops when she feels my piercing. Her eyes widen, and a wicked smile spreads across her lips. I run my tongue piercings over my bottom lip and pull it between my teeth.

"I've never seen one like this before," she says, moving closer to look at it.

"It's not a common one. They call it the triangle piercing because it provides stimulation to the clit from the back and on both sides."

The bed dips between my legs as Adrestia climbs onto it. She settles, spreading me open wider, and I lift my head the best I can to look down at her, only to find her licking her lips. Her pupils are blown wide as she looks up at me. She maintains eye contact with me as she lowers her mouth to my pussy, drawing the tip of her tongue excruciatingly slow up my soaked center. When she reaches my clit, she stops to play with my piercing. I buck my hips and cry out at the contact.

Just as fast as she started, she's sitting up. I whimper and try to move my legs, needing more, but they won't budge, so I groan out in frustration.

She's got herself on her haunches, wiping off her mouth using the back of her hand with a damn smirk on her face. "You taste so fucking delicious, but as much as I want more, I have plans for you right now. Be a good girl and don't move." I huff out a breath, and she smacks my clit again. "Patience, little one."

"Do you not remember me telling you that word isn't in my vocabulary?"

"Well, you're going to learn it today," she says, climbing off the bed with that smirk still on her lips.

I pull at the ropes on each of my extremities out of pure desperation. None of them move. What makes matters worse is that Adrestia has my legs tied so far apart I can't even rub my thighs together. This is torture, and I am *not* a fan. I guess that's the point, though.

The lioness comes to stand beside me, placing some things on the bed. I can't turn my head far enough to see what's there, but I feel like she did that on purpose.

"Eyes on me," she demands. I do as I'm told, and she praises me. "Good girl."

I immediately melt into a metaphorical puddle because why wouldn't I? Being called a 'good girl' *and* having a woman as beautiful as the one before me saying 'eyes on me' is the hottest thing ever. There's not much else that tops that.

Well, maybe if there were more than one of her. Hmm, I've never experimented with multiple partners, and now I'm curious.

Focusing back on the woman before me, I watch as she slowly undresses herself before me. By the time she lifts her shirt over her head, my pussy is throbbing, and there's nothing I can do to relieve it.

When everything is finally on the floor, she grabs whatever it is she put on the bed and climbs up between my parted legs again. Her teeth worry her bottom lip as she stares down at the items in her hand. Now that I can see it, my heart stutters in my chest. The toy in her hands looks to be a double-ended vibrator—I can see the buttons from where I lie. One end curves up with a semi-bulbous tip, while the other end extends mostly straight out.

She pops the top off a bottle of lube and coats the curved tip. "Have you ever seen one of these?"

"N-no. Well, not in person at least."

"They're a lot of fun. I think you'll really enjoy it," she says with another smile playing at the corner of her lips.

I stay quiet, just watching her. She amazes me, especially with the fact that she's always smiling or making jokes, even though she's clearly been through a lot; the faint scars on her arms and sides speak to that.

My gaze drifts down to her breasts while she continues prepping the toy. Even with as muscular as she is, she's got some really nice tits. They're really perky—almost picture perfect—and not overly big for my small hands. Her sun-kissed skin, which amazingly shows no sign of tan lines anywhere, is the perfect contrast to her reddish-brown nipples. Through each peak is a silver barbell that most would consider boring, but I couldn't disagree more; they're so fucking sexy to me.

She draws my attention back to her when she tosses the bottle of lube back on the bed. Our eyes meet as she lowers the toy between her legs. I try to lift my head so I can watch her, but I'm tied down so tight I can't see that far down. My gaze flies back to her face when she sharply inhales. She's got her head thrown back, eyes closed, and lips parted, pushing her chest out even further. It's hot as fuck.

After a moment, her eyes open back up—they're nearly black because her pupils have taken over almost her whole golden iris—and return to mine. I'm caught off guard when her tail swishes up behind her. She takes that opportunity to fully seat the toy inside me with one swift movement, causing me to gasp and arch my back.

"This is about the only time I wish I had a dick of my own, but at least I've got this going for me," she says, her tail slithering between us so it can play with my nipple.

That's a new one for me.

I'm so distracted by her tail that I don't notice her pressing one of the buttons on the toy until it begins vibrating. A shudder rips through me, and I can't keep myself from moaning. The vibrations spread all through my body, and fuck do they feel good.

"Do you like that?" she asks, thrusting her hips until our pubic bones meet. I moan loudly again and nod my head, but she smacks my breast. "Use your words, little one."

The toy slides out of me as her hips pull back, and I immediately miss the fullness. "Yes, lioness. I fucking love it. Keep going. Please," I whimper.

"Such a good girl," she says, thrusting her hips again and plunging the toy inside me until it hits my G-spot.

"Oh, fuck," I cry out and arch my back, which pulls on my tied wrists. While I'm loving that she has me tied up, I wish I weren't so that I could touch her. I want to dig my nails into her back, leaving my mark so she can see just how much I'm loving this for the next few days to come.

Her hands come to massage my breasts as she continues pumping her hips. My moans and screams get louder with each thrust, and I know I'm not going to last much longer. Then she leans forward, sending me into another damn dimension. In this position, our clits rub together, and it has me coming so hard that I'm sure people miles around could hear me scream.

She lowers her mouth to my neck, kissing up to my ear. "I wish I could feel how fucking tight your cunt is right now, strangling this toy like a good little slut. Maybe next time I'll fuck you with my tail so I *can* feel it," she whispers with one last kiss on my neck before she bites me and lets out a growl.

If I weren't already coming, that right there would've done it. I love being degraded during sex. Most of the time, that's the only way I can get off—especially with men.

"I love the way you fuck me, lioness. Fuck, I wish I could touch you right now," I say.

She balances herself on one hand as she continues her thrusts and loosens one of my wrists. Once it's loose, she goes back to what she was doing.

"Just one?" I whine, still breathing heavily.

"Do you want me to tie it back up?" she asks, panting.

I give her a Cheshire grin and bring my hand to her throat, grabbing it tightly. "I only need one. There are just fewer options." Her eyes roll into the back of her head, and her thrusts stutter. I huff out a laugh and squeeze harder. "Keep going, sweetheart. Fuck me rough and hard, or however the hell you want. Use me like the little slut I am. Make yourself come all over my pussy."

With that, she starts pounding into me. Her throat bobbing below my hand when she tries to swallow. She's so fucking beautiful that I catch myself just staring at her while she fucks me. It feels good, but I want to know what it'd be like to force her to her knees and make her do whatever I want her to.

Her mouth falls open with a loud moan. I know she's getting close, so I thrust into her—to the best of my ability—and wait for her to come undone above me.

Chapter Seven

ADRESTIA

This whole experience with Vaelyn tops every other experience I've had with another woman. I've always loved to dominate, but I'm enjoying this harpy topping from the bottom. I'm half tempted to untie her so she can just dominate me because I'm so fucking close with her hand around my throat, and her clit piercing rubbing against mine is providing the perfect friction on my swollen clit. I got mine pierced eons ago—at least that's what it feels like. Mine is just what they call a VCH, or vertical clitoral hood. It provides some damn good sensations to my clit, but adding Vaelyn's triangle piercing in the mix is fucking bliss.

Now that she's thrusting into me, it's making my side of the vibrator go deeper, and I can't hold on any longer. An intense orgasm crashes through me so hard I nearly pass out. I usually don't make a lot of noise when I'm having sex, but this climax is unlike any I've had before, and I can't stop the screams coming from my lips.

"Those sounds are so fucking pretty coming from your perfect lips. Ride the wave," she whispers below me.

"Holy fuck," I pant, finally coming down from my high. "That was... unbelievable."

Her hand massages my throat lightly before she drops it down to the bed. "That's definitely a word for it."

I have to give myself a moment to catch my breath before I'm able to sit up and take care of the toy. When I finally pull it from my pussy, my walls are still fluttering wildly. I'm not sure if it's like this because it wants more or if it's just me coming down from my high.

I'm about to climb off the bed when she grabs my wrist. "Give it here. I want to taste you, and I refuse to let this deliciousness go to waste. Look at how soaked it is."

My eyes drift to the side of the toy that had been inside me. I'm shocked to see that my arousal is literally dripping off the end. I've never come so hard in my life.

Looking between her legs, I see a huge wet spot. Did I squirt? Or is that from her?

I roll my lip between my teeth and bring the toy closer until it's just out of reach from her mouth. "You're going to have to beg me for it, little one," I whisper and then dart my tongue out to lap up her arousal on the toy. When her taste hits my tongue, I savor its complexity—starting tart like cherries, but followed closely by a rich sweetness like pomegranates. I'm already obsessed after only two tastes, causing a growl to rumble in my chest. My need for her is building, and I'm dying to fuck her again.

Her hand snakes into my hair and grabs a handful. "Untie me. Let me eat your pussy. You still haven't let me taste you."

I tsk. "I'd rather take this toy and fuck you again. That was one of my top ten orgasms of all time."

"Is that so? Maybe you can untie me and let *me* fuck *you* with that toy instead. How about that?"

My pussy clenches at her suggestion, making me want to take her up on that offer. Instead, I throw the toy to the side and crash my lips to hers. She slides her tongue into my mouth, tangling it with mine. Both of us groan. We've only just met this evening, but I don't think I'll ever be able to get enough of her; I already don't want her to leave this apartment.

Shifting my position, I throw one of my legs over her so I'm straddling her thigh and grind my sensitive pussy against it. Then, I reach up to untie her other arm. Once the rope falls away, her arms wrap around my neck, and she digs her nails into my shoulders. I groan into her mouth before pulling back to untie her legs. As I push back from her, she drags her nails—no, her talons—down my arms. Little dots of blood appear as they continue their descent. I fucking love how wet it makes me.

When I sit up, I grind my hips against hers and rub our clits together. Vaelyn moans weakly below me.

"That was such a weak moan," I say, rocking my hips again. "Am I not giving you enough?"

She shakes her head and tries to sneak her hand between us. I grab it before she can squeeze in, tsking at her.

"Please," she whimpers.

I abandon the thought of untying her ankles and pin her hands back above her head. "Do I need to re-tie your hands? You *will* take what I give you, and you *will not* get yourself off when you think it's not enough. Do you understand?"

She nods, and I grind my hips against hers again. The angle I'm at puts the best kind of friction on my clit, and I surprise myself when I gasp at the same time she does. Apparently, I need more too, so I do it a few more times.

When I pause, she tries to buck her hips, and I shake my head. I shift both of her hands into one of mine and bring my other to her throat, digging my fingers into her pulse points. "If you keep testing me, I'll flip you over and tie you down so you can't move at all. Then I'll spank your ass until you're raw and edge you to the point where release is all you can think about. I'll have you begging me to get you off, but I won't. Instead, I'll leave you on this bed until I feel you've learned your lesson. Is that what you want, little one?"

She rolls her tongue piercings over her bottom lip as she licks it. "Not particularly at the moment. I'd rather have my turn to dominate you."

"Maybe later. Right now, I really do love torturing you."

One of her eyebrows raises. "You realize I could easily flip you over, even with my legs still being tied, right?"

I scoff. "You're nearly half my size. There's no—"

Her eyes narrow at me as a devious smile curves her lips. In the next second, she's pulled her hands from beneath mine and has me on my back, just as she threatened.

"I may be small, but I am much stronger than you realize," she says, lowering her face to mine and kissing the tip of my nose.

"Lesson learned," I whisper and then reach out to grasp her neck, pulling her mouth back to mine.

She reaches back to release her legs from their bindings as we kiss. Once she's freed from her bindings, she realigns our centers and rocks her hips into mine. I moan into her mouth, enjoying how good it feels to have her on top of me, taking control of me.

When she finds a good rhythm, I start rocking my hips against hers. Her movements become erratic within a minute, and I know she's close to release. Doing as she'd done to me, I bring my free hand to her shoulder and elongate my talons slightly. Then, I drag them down her arm, watching as her blood races my talons to her wrist.

Her lips leave mine, and she places our foreheads together, breathing heavily. "Fuck, that feels like heaven."

I turn my head to the side, catching a droplet of her blood with my tongue. "Soak my pussy with your cum, little one. I know you're close. Come for me."

She cries out, her mouth falling to my neck, where she buries herself. I lap up the blood running down her arm and pull my talons back in. She lets out one last moan before her orgasm sweeps over her. I'm not far behind, crashing over the precipice with one more roll of my hips.

Through ragged breaths, she sits up and says, "Holy fuck. I've never come so hard just by scissoring."

I rub my hands up and down her back for a moment before I pull her down to kiss me. "You have to have the right partner—one that knows what they're doing."

"You clearly do."

With a sly smirk, I say, "Let's just say I've been around the block a time or two... or many more than that. Let's go take a shower to get all this blood and sweat off us."

She plays with one of her tongue piercings. "I really should get going."

I shake my head. "You can stay for a while; I don't mind. I actually rather enjoy your being here."

She rolls her eyes. "I'm pretty sure it's the sex you liked, not my company."

When she tries to sit up, I hold on to her so she can't move. "The sex was very enjoyable, but that's not why I want you to stay. I spend so much time alone; It's nice to have someone to talk to, at least for a while."

An emotion I can't place flickers across her face, but it's gone all too quickly. "Fine. Let's go shower."

I smile and smack her ass. She lets out a yelp that turns to a moan, and I laugh. Then I sit up and point to the door opposite the one we came in. "That's the bathroom. Let me grab some towels, and I'll be right in."

She nods and heads for the bathroom while I head for my closet. A couple of minutes later, I join her. When I open the door, steam greets me first, telling me she's already started the shower, and she likes it when the water's hot, which is good because I do too. My gaze drifts to where she stands in the shower. All I can see is her silhouette because the majority of the glass is frosted, and she's just short enough that the top of her head is the only part of her that's visible. I'm still surprised at how strong she is, considering her size. I wonder if it has to do with being a harpy or if it's something else altogether.

Either way, I clear my head and step inside to deposit the towels on the counter so I can join her. When I get closer, I realize she's humming something and stop for a moment to listen. It's a song I instantly recognize because it's one of my favorites: "Caramel" by Sleep Token.

"That's a beautiful song," I say, stepping into the shower behind her.

She nearly jumps out of her skin. "Holy fuck. You scared the shit out of me!"

"Did you not hear me come into the bathroom?"

"No!"

I shake my head. "It's not like I was quiet, and I know I didn't take that long getting towels."

She sighs. "I'm just always inside my own head."

"Well, let's get cleaned off, and then we can go watch a movie or a TV show. How does that sound?"

"I haven't watched TV or seen a movie in years," she mumbles, staring down at the black tile floor of my shower.

Bringing my fingers to her chin, I tilt it up to make her look at me. "What's wrong, little one?"

She shakes her head, the little she can with the way I'm holding onto her. "I've been alone for a long time and haven't found a place I'm comfortable settling, so I haven't partaken in a lot of the normal things others do on a daily basis."

"I'm sorry. Can I ask why?"

Her tongue rings clack against her teeth. "I didn't feel like I belonged in my nest. Other than that, I don't feel comfortable talking about it—I don't even know you."

"And yet you were comfortable enough to come into my home and expose yourself to me," I say, and then stop myself from saying anything else. "I'm sorry. That was uncalled for."

"You have valid points, but I'm comfortable in my own body, and I'm capable of taking care of myself. I'm not comfortable talking in depth about how my life was in the nest before I left."

I let go of her chin and take a step back. "That's understandable. I'm sorry."

She shrugs. "It's in our nature to be curious. It's also in our nature to question things that don't make sense to us."

"That doesn't mean I had to be rude."

With a nod, she tips her head back and lets the water run through her hair. I reach over to my wall shelf, grab my loofah, and pour some of my body wash on it. Then I lather up the soap and take another step toward her.

I place my hand on her hip, reminding her I'm here. She wipes the water from her face as she looks at me.

"May I?" I ask, lifting the loofah so she can see it.

She nods, and a wave of relief washes over me. I bring the loofah to her neck, swiping it across her skin in gentle strokes. Her head falls back, and a moan slips past her lips. I bite my lip, but continue, making sure to get her clean while I still try to admire her beautiful body.

When I'm done with her upper body, I quickly clean her lower body. I want to make her feel special—and not just in a sexual way. It's one of the things I miss the most about my relationship with Avyanna. She'd been alone for hundreds of years, but she still knew how to make me feel like I meant something to her.

Even though I don't know this woman, I want her to know she's special. And, weirdly enough, I don't want her to leave. I want her to stay with me because, for the first time since my relationship with Avyanna, I feel like I might be able to let someone else in again.

Chapter Eight

When I wake up, I'm not exactly sure where I am, but I know I feel safe. Thinking back, all I remember from last night was the hunter lying me down on a bed and undressing me before I passed out. Where the hell is she now?

I lie there for a minute, but my bladder screams at me to use the bathroom, so I hurry in and out because I'm still naked as the day I was born. After coming out, I try to find some clothes, which is useless because the hunter doesn't have many clothes, and the ones I can find don't really look like they'll fit me. A few minutes in, I just give up, grabbing the sheet from the bed and wrapping it around me.

The smell of pancakes hits my nostrils the moment I open the bedroom door, and my stomach grumbles—I'm not even sure of the last time I ate right now. I plod down the hallway toward the smell without thought. As much as I want to look around, I'm curious to see what the hunter is up to.

At the end of the hall, I come to an open archway, which leads to a barren living room. I don't even remember us going through it last night, but since there wasn't anything in it, the fact that it's not familiar doesn't surprise me.

To my right is a half-wall that looks into the kitchen. On the other side of that wall stands the hunter with her back to me, and I'm hypnotized by the sight of her. Her ethereally pale skin is a stark contrast to her wavy, black hair, which she has wound into a bun at the crown of her head. The sunlight peeking through the window to her left shines off her silky hair, revealing crimson streaks throughout. My hands itch to take her hair down, to run my fingers through the strands, and see just how soft it is.

When she shifts her stance, my gaze is drawn down to her powerful shoulders and back. She's only wearing a spaghetti strap shirt, so I can see all the muscles flex as she flips the pancakes that drew me out here. A tattoo that resembles a snake winds from the nape of her neck over her right shoulder and disappears out of my sight. The outline is all in black, but the scales appear to be emerald green, similar to the color of my snakes in my gorgon form. I'm curious to see the rest of it.

"Good morning, my little relic. Are you enjoying the view?" she asks, catching me off guard.

"Sorry. I didn't mean—"

She shakes her head. "There's no need to apologize. I'm making breakfast, but I'm sure you already knew that—these pancakes do smell pretty amazing. I've tried not to eat too many of them. Although it took every ounce of my control not to eat you for breakfast this morning, too."

I blush and stumble over my words. "Thanks for making breakfast. Where, uh, are my clothes?"

She turns toward me with a pan in hand and drops it directly into the sink that's positioned under the half-wall opening. "I'm washing them. You're welcome to borrow some of mine. They're all still packed up, so they can be tricky to find, but I'm not sure how well my bottoms will fit. You were definitely blessed in the ass department far more than I was. Or... you could wear nothing at all. I'm quite fine with that, too."

With a nervous laugh, I begin my walk back down the hall, and she calls out, "Breakfast will be ready when you get back out here."

Thankfully, I'm able to find clothes relatively quickly once I've figured out where things are. I go through three pairs of shorts before I can find ones I'm able to squeeze into, and I curse her for being right about my ass. When I'm done, I head back out to the living room. The hunter is standing with her back to me again in the kitchen, but she turns toward me rather quickly this time.

She looks me up and down as she waves me in. "I see you were able to find something. Your breakfast is here on the table. Come, sit."

My stomach grumbles, reminding me just how hungry I am, and I internally scold it as I make my way into the kitchen. To the left, under another window, is a small, round table with one chair and a plate of food.

"Where's yours?" I ask.

She waves me off, and I sit. "I ate a little bit while I was waiting for you, but being what I am, I don't require much in the way of 'normal food'."

My brows furrow. "And what exactly *are* you?"

She sighs. "I walked right into that. My kind are called a lot of things; I think doppelgänger and mimic are the ones I prefer most."

I choke on the food I was just about to swallow. When she moves to help me, I hold out my hand and take a sip of the milk she'd given me. After clearing my throat a few times, I look up at her. "You're a skinwalker?"

A growl rumbles in her chest. "I fucking hate that term."

My heart sinks into my stomach. "I'm sorry. That's the way I've always heard your kind referred to."

"It's not your fault," she says, pausing for a deep breath. "I apologize for that visceral reaction. The term brings up a lot of bad memories."

I take a bite of my food and nod. "So, being a doppelgänger must be useful in your line of work, I assume."

"It's helpful for sure and also likely how I've lived so long."

Clearing my throat, I wipe any excess crumbs from my face. "May I ask how old you are?"

She laughs. "Let's just say I'm a *hell* of a lot older than I look, Roxanna."

I cringe. "Please just call me Roxi. Roxanna is so formal and makes me feel like I'm in trouble or something."

A beautiful smile lights up her face. "Roxi suits you."

I blush and take another bite of my food. "How do you know my name? I know you're a hunter, but you said you weren't after me."

She sighs and rubs her hand over her face. "One of my assignments was for one of your father's guards. That's when I first saw you. I abandoned my assignment and watched you for several days before I almost lost control of myself and had to… feed. When I went back to check on you, everything and everyone were gone. After that, I did everything in my power to find out who you were."

"Do you remember who you were hunting?"

She takes a moment to think. "I'm pretty sure his name was Calen." My heart skips a beat, and my face must show my shock because her brows furrow. "I'm going to guess you're familiar with him."

Placing my fork on my plate, I stumble over my words. "Y-yeah, I was."

Her jaw ticks. "How familiar with him were you?"

I bite my lip. "He's the one who took my virginity. My father killed him as a warning of what would happen if the guards touched me again and as a punishment for my putting his guards in danger."

Skin rippling, she growls, "Apparently, you have a habit of attracting disgusting men."

My mouth pops open. "Excuse me?"

She takes a step toward me, and my glamour drops, but that doesn't stop her from crowding my space. "Both of the men you've allowed to touch you have been rapists and murderers. Hell, most of the men your father employed to guard you over the years were shitty people—although your father was a questionable man himself, so it doesn't surprise me with the company he kept. I just wish he had done better to keep his daughter safe."

Her bringing up my choice in the men I let touch me feels like a punch to the gut. I can't deny that Merric was a bad guy, but I suppose I didn't know enough about Calen, or any of the other guards my father employed, well enough to say what kind of men they were.

Who my father was is a whole other story. I never knew what he did outside our home, but I knew exactly the man he was around me. He'd told me numerous times while I was growing up that I was a disappointment and that I'd destroyed his life when I was born. He blamed me for my mother's death, even though it wasn't truly my fault.

Her labor with me was hard on her body. Back then, things were very different from what they are now. There were no ultrasound machines or heart rate monitors for the baby in the mother's womb. My mother spent three days laboring at home with a midwife checking on her periodically before she began to bleed profusely. My father rushed her to the hospital, insisting there was something wrong. They took her back quickly and were about to do a cesarean section when my mother felt me coming out. The doctor positioned himself between her legs just in time to catch me, but then his eyes met mine, and he turned to stone.

My father was the first to notice something was wrong. For whatever reason, the nurses weren't around, so my father called out for help because my mom was still bleeding. It took too long for another doctor to arrive, but there wasn't much they could've done—she'd already lost far too much blood.

When my father finally got to hold me, he refused to look into my eyes, knowing the curse placed on his family nearly a millennium before had finally presented itself. My father never did tell me about the curse before he passed. The staff in the houses we occupied over the years explained that the curse was the reason he hid me away from the world.

Everyone knows gorgons are dangerous, and as much as I was a disappointment to him, I was his daughter, so I took solace in knowing he tried to protect me. Or who knows, maybe he was protecting everyone else by keeping me from going out and inadvertently turning others to stone.

I settle back in my chair and cross my arms over my chest. "I can't help that I crave attention—I never got any growing up because of what I am. So, forgive me for getting attention from the men who would give it to me. Instead, blame my father for never giving me what I deserved."

She takes a deep breath, and the rippling of her skin slows until it stops altogether. Then, she takes a step away from me. "I can understand that. I'm sorry."

I shrug my shoulders. "What do you really want, doppelgänger?"

Her nose scrunches. "I don't like your calling me that. My name is Avyanna."

Rolling my eyes, I say, "Fine, Avyanna. What do you want with me?"

"We've already established this," she says with an exasperated sigh.

"Because I make you feel... different? That doesn't make sense to me in the least."

"When you've lived as long as I have, seen as much as I have, and experienced as much as I have, you become desensitized. Only one other person has made me feel something over the last few centuries besides pain and hatred toward the world that robbed me of so much of my life. One look at you, and I was obsessed. I can't explain it, and I'm not completely sure why yet, but I have to know what's different about you."

My brows slam down. "Okay, but what if that's not what *I* want? What if I just want to go home?"

A dark laugh leaves her lips. "You don't want to go back to being caged. You made that *very* clear last night when I told you I was bringing you here."

"My family has several places I can stay," I counter.

"Your father's men will find you at any of his homes, and you know that."

I shake my head. "There's no way I can stay with you. I don't even know you."

"You know my name, and you know what I am. There aren't many others who can say they do."

"What little I know about your kind isn't anything good, hence why I only know of you all as skinwalkers. Your kind are the things of nightmares to most supes."

Her lip curls. "My kind is nearly extinct, all thanks to the fear surrounding what we can do."

I raise my hands in defense. "I'm just telling you what I know, which, like I said, isn't much. It does little to ease my fear of you."

A wicked smile lifts the corner of her lips. "You weren't so scared of me last night when I undressed you and lay beside you while we were both naked."

My face flushes. "I was exhausted and could barely keep my eyes open! Plus, I didn't even know you climbed into the bed with me."

She raises an eyebrow. "I could also smell your arousal this morning while I was making breakfast, right before I turned around to greet you. You weren't so scared then."

My mouth drops to the floor. "I was, uh, admiring the view. And I didn't know what you were then."

"Tell yourself whatever you'd like so you can sleep at night."

I clench my jaw. "I still don't know you."

"We have all the time in the world, my little relic. We're both immortal after all."

Chapter Nine

Avyanna

I let Roxi finish her breakfast in peace and wander off to check on her clothes. I'd just thrown them in the dryer before I started on her food, so I'm certain they're dry now. My walk to the washer and dryer takes me past my bedroom, and I stop at the doorway. Her scent assaults my nostrils, beckoning me to drown myself in it.

Giving in to temptation, I stroll in and bury my face in the sheet she'd wrapped herself in this morning. Her intoxicating scent fills my nostrils, one that reminds me of night-blooming jasmine. But then something more earthy and grounding carries into it, like vetiver. Now, I don't want to put this sheet down or leave my bedroom. The only thing that would be better is having her arousal coating my tongue or her blood filling my mouth.

Wetness soaks the insides of my thighs, and I throw the sheet down, trying to clear my mind of her. I can't afford to get lost in the thoughts of what I want to do to her yet. If I do, I won't be able to keep myself from losing control.

Stalking into the closet, I shuffle through my clothes, still stuffed in boxes. When I find something comfortable, I throw it on and go to check on Roxi's clothes. Thankfully, they're dry, so I take them back to my bed for her when she's ready.

As I set her clothes down, the sound of a faucet trickles down the hall. I tiptoe out to follow the sound, which leads me toward the kitchen. Over the half wall, I watch as Roxi stands at the sink... washing the dishes?

She's returned to her human form, her straight black hair thrown over one of her shoulders, cascading toward the water, but she seems unfazed by it. Unlike in her gorgon form, where her skin is ashen and mottled like the stone she can turn others to, her porcelain-like skin glistens, reminding me of a stone that's been recently polished. Something in me wants to stroke my fingers over it to see how it feels. But as she looks down, her cute, narrow snub nose twitches, almost like she's going to sneeze. It takes everything in me not to giggle at the sight.

I'm caught off guard by that thought because I can't remember the last time I *giggled*. This woman is a sight to behold. In such a short time, she's breaking down the walls I've built to protect myself from the pain I've come to accept when it comes to others.

"Are you just going to stand there and stare at me with that wicked smile on your face, or are you going to get in here and help me clean?" she asks, startling me.

"Hey, I cooked. That means you clean," I say with a playful lilt in my voice.

"I guess I'd better pick up cooking so you can be the one to clean next time."

"Next time?" I ask, brow raised. "Does that mean you don't plan to run off?"

Her cheeks pinken, and she looks back down into the sink. "I don't have much of a choice, do I?"

"Not really. If you run, I *will* catch you. And when I do, I'll do as I please with you." As the words leave my lips, the scent of her arousal overwhelms me, and I tsk. "Be careful with that. I'm already having a hard time keeping my hands off you. Your arousal—when I'm too close—will have me losing control in no time. Trust me when I say that's not something you want right now."

She bites her lip and attempts to return to washing the dishes. "I can't help it. I've never done anything like this, especially not with a woman, and I'm *very* intrigued. What makes it even better is that you can look me in the eye when you do what you want to me. Plus, I have a feeling that you'd respect my wishes if I told you to stop."

I grin as I stalk toward the half wall. Her eyes return to me, and I look directly into the emerald pools. "You think too highly of me. I don't know if I'd be able to stop once I get my hands on you."

"Well, if it makes you feel any better, I don't think I'd tell you to stop. Even if that's what I truly wanted. Because I want you so fucking bad that I'd let my body override my brain."

As I reach the wall, I grab onto the ledge tightly. "And that's why I'm trying to keep a good hold on my control. If I need to go out and feed just so I don't lose it around you, I will."

She drops the dishes into the sink and steps toward the archway, causing my heart to skip a beat. "What if I want you to lose control?"

I feel my pupils constrict, honing in on her like she's my prey, as my monster starts to take over. My grip tightens on the ledge, crumbling the drywall just to keep myself in place. "If I lose control, I might hurt you, and I won't let that happen."

Once she reaches the archway, my eyes drift down her body. She looks perfect in my clothes. The high-rise shorts she chose pull snugly over her large ass, making my mouth water. And the crop top she found cuts off right below her breasts, showing off just a little bit of skin above the waistband on the shorts.

She laughs, a melodic sound, drawing my attention back up to her eyes. "Pain mixes well with pleasure, from what I've heard."

"This pain will have you flirting with death if I can't control myself enough," I growl.

"You wouldn't allow me to die."

"What makes you so confident of that?" I ask, genuinely curious to hear what she has to say.

"You have yet to understand why I make you feel different, and I know you won't let me die until you figure it out."

A snarl creeps up my chest, and I'm in front of her in an instant, grabbing her throat. I slam her back against a wall, crowding her space, as a voice I don't recognize leaves me. "I'd much rather die than let anything happen to you. If anyone so much as lays a finger on you, they'll lose at least that finger if not far, *far* more."

Her scent consumes me, arousal coursing through her at an intense rate, and I'm struggling not to slide my hand between her perfect thighs, to feel how wet she is. "You're going to be the absolute death of me, my little relic."

"Do it. Kiss me. Touch me, Avyanna. I want you to lose control."

My resolve snaps, and my lips crash onto hers. She moans into my mouth as I release her neck, moving my hands down to her thighs. I lift her off the floor, and she wraps herself around me. Having her in my arms like this feels like a heaven I know I don't deserve.

Without having to look, I take her back to the bedroom and lay her on the bed, breaking our kiss so I can trail light kisses across her jaw to her neck. Her legs unravel from around my waist, while her hands tangle in my hair, not wanting to let me go yet. The most delicious sounds leave her lips, urging me along.

I lift my lips from her skin for a moment and whisper, "I need you to tell me if I'm hurting you or if you're feeling drained at all. Once I start taking from you, it's going to be hard for me to stop."

Her back bows. "As long as you keep going, you can have as much as you want."

"Roxi," I growl.

She whines and fists my hair, trying to push my lips back to her skin. "Please keep going."

"Fuck. Just... tell me if I'm hurting you."

"Fine," she grumbles.

My lips return to her neck, and my canines elongate, dying to sink into her flesh. Surprise flickers through me when I'm able to stop myself from giving in to the urge. Sliding my hands under her shirt, I palm her breasts for a moment before I encourage her to sit up and pull the shirt off.

A groan rumbles in my throat. "Your body is fucking perfection."

She rolls her eyes and falls back against the bed. "I'm sure you've seen better in your lifetime."

I shake my head, running my fingertips over her smooth skin, making her shiver. "None of them has ever compared to yours."

"Whatever you say."

The corner of my lips tips up. "You're learning quickly."

"I just want you to keep going. It feels so good when you touch me—unlike anything I've ever felt before."

My fingers reach the hem of her shorts, and I slip them under the band, playing with the sensitive skin there. "This is just the beginning."

"Get on with it then."

"Watch that mouth," I say, my gaze turning severe.

"What are you going to do if I don't?"

I hum and lean down to whisper in her ear. "I'll start by tying you up, putting a vibrator in your pussy on the lowest setting—which we know won't get you close in the least—and making you watch as I get myself off."

She bites her lip as she looks into my eyes. "Is that all?"

"Depends on how much of a brat you want to be."

She bucks her hips and tries to grind her core against me.

I tsk. "You're being very naughty."

"I'm very impatient. Don't act like you don't want this as much as I do right now."

"I hate that you already know that's true."

Her hands slide under my shirt, and she glides her fingers over my skin like I'd done to her earlier. A moan slips past my lips while my eyes slam shut, focusing on the feel of her skin against mine.

"Fuck, that feels so good," I whimper.

When her hands reach my breasts, she tries to grab one in each hand, but fails—my breasts being bigger than her hands can handle—so she pinches my nipples between her thumb and forefinger, playing with my piercings. I gasp and lean into her touch because it's been so fucking long since someone has played with me like this.

I'm so lost in lust that I don't realize Roxi has changed into her gorgon form until her snakes' tongues flick over my face. My eyes fly open and meet her slitted emerald ones. Every time I see them, I fear the worst will happen, but I know now that there's a connection between us, allowing me to look her in the eye.

Her tongue sweeps over her lips. "I want to taste you."

"I was supposed to be the one pleasing you, not the other way around. But I kind of want to be selfish and let you do it; I haven't allowed anyone else to touch me for decades."

Her hands grip my hips, and in a rush of movement I can barely comprehend, I'm on my back. She wastes little time ripping my clothes off until I lie before her bare. Her snakes slither back and forth across her head, flicking their tongues out as they eye me like the biggest feast they've ever been presented with.

A wicked grin spreads across her lips. "They're eager to help me please you. They forced themselves out to do so. I've never had that happen, but it's not like I've ever had the opportunity to do something like this before, either. There's something about you that makes me feral too, Avyanna."

"Fucking hell," I whisper as she lowers her lips to my neck. Pleasure shoots through me, and I arch my back, never wanting her to stop. When she reaches my breast, her tongue darts out to lick my nipple and play with the piercing while one of her snakes takes the other one into its mouth and bites down. I yelp in surprise, but it quickly turns to a moan.

Her other snakes snap and hiss at each other, trying like hell to get to me. Their involvement is intriguing, making it feel like I have multiple partners vying for my attention. Let's just say I'm not complaining about it in the least.

As one snake releases my nipple, another clamps onto it. I sharply inhale and fist my hands in the sheets. Roxi huffs out a laugh against my skin just as the second snake lets go of my stiff peak. Her tongue trails across my chest, taking my battered nipple in her mouth. She lets out an appreciative hum and sucks on it harder, nearly sucking my soul out through it.

Her teeth run over my flesh as she releases the suction, my nipple leaving her mouth with an audible pop, and I let out a relieved sigh. Looking down at her, I watch, confused, as her forked tongue darts out to lick her bloodied lips. Then realization hits, and my gaze flies down to my breast. Four tiny blood drops sit side by side, which look like they're bite marks from her snakes. Above those are two larger wounds that sit further apart—just the right distance between where Roxi's canines are. The skin there is torn slightly, and blood trickles across my chest from them, collecting between my breasts.

"Sorry, they're a little blood thirsty and I had to have a taste for myself," she says, wiping the back of her hand across her mouth.

I quirk a brow at her. "You drink blood?"

She shrugs. "On occasion, I've been able to. I don't need it to survive, but it'll give me a boost depending on what kind of creature I'm drinking from."

"Does my blood make you feel any different?"

Her eyes slide closed for a moment before she's peering back at me through her lashes. "I'm more in tune with you, but that's about it."

"How interesting. I learn something new every once in a while."

"There aren't many of my kind left in the world, so I'm sure you don't know much about us either."

"I was actually around during the peak of the gorgons, and I've taken down a few in my time, so I know more than you think."

Her brows furrow. "Just how old are you?"

"Everything I just told you should give you some hints," I say, trying to sit up.

She shoves me back down onto the bed, keeping her hand on my sternum. "Don't deflect. I'm not done with you."

"Then I suggest you get on with it."

Her slitted pupils constrict, and she keeps eye contact with me as she bends down to lick up the last of the blood on my chest. "You started asking questions, which interrupted me."

"Well, by all means, continue."

The snakes atop her head hiss and snap at me again—feisty little things, just like the woman they accompany. She scoots further down on the bed and lowers herself onto her forearms between my thighs, ass high in the air, wiggling as she looks me over.

My pussy throbs under her gaze, begging for her to touch it. She licks her lips, and the soft pads of her fingers slide across my folds to spread me open. One of her knuckles grazes over my clit in the process, nearly sending me flying off the bed.

"Sensitive, are we?" she asks, voice full of lust.

I nod frantically, biting down on my lip, and she does it again. Unable to stop myself, I whimper.

Her tongue licks up my slit, and she moans. "You're so fucking wet, Vee. And you taste so sweet."

The only word I can get out of my mouth is 'more' because that's all I want right now. It's been far too long since someone has pleased me, and I *need* her to continue.

She huffs out a quiet laugh, which has her warm breath flitting across my sensitive clit. I bow my back, and she dives in, sinking her forked tongue deep into me. A strangled cry leaves my lips as I fist my hands in the sheets again. That only serves to encourage her, making her tongue split inside me until she finds my G-spot.

"Fuck," I whimper, hips moving of their own accord as she fucks me with her decadent tongue.

Then her snakes join in the fun. One of them latches onto my clit while another wiggles itself toward my ass, flicking its tongue over my tight hole. I've never let anyone play with me there, but if that's what this woman wants, I'll let her do it. All the sensations have me writhing beneath her; I'm already so close.

Her tongue slips out of me, but her snakes don't stop their pursuits. "Come on my tongue, Vee. Drown me in your delicious arousal."

My eyes roll back and my toes curl as she slides her tongue back in, splitting it to toy with the walls of my pussy. It's all becoming so overwhelming, but I'm tipped over the edge when the snake on my clit releases my sensitive bundle of nerves and another bites down harder, suctioning onto the area. I scream my release, slamming my eyes shut. When spots dance across my vision, I fear I'm going to pass out.

Roxi lets me ride out my orgasm before she and her snakes release their hold on me. I'm a shaking mess, unable to do anything but breathe while this beautiful woman kisses her way up my body. When she reaches my neck, I turn my face to capture her lips. We kiss for what feels like hours, but is probably only minutes at the most.

She pulls back, needing to come up for air. Her hooded eyes fixate on mine, and we stay there, staring at each other while we breathe heavily.

"I really want to stay in this bed all day with you, but I would also love to get some stuff from my father's house," she whispers.

My brows furrow. "What do you need? I'll get it for you. I won't let your father's men take you from me again."

"I mean, I need clothes and the like more than anything."

"We can buy you new stuff. I don't want you going back there," I growl.

She tenses her jaw. "What happened to not keeping me locked up?"

I sigh. "We can go out and buy things, but I don't want you going back to that house."

One of her eyebrows raises. "And how are we going to manage that with my stone-turning gaze?"

"Fuck. I forgot about that, weirdly enough. Let me find some sunglasses or something for you."

"Sunglasses don't help inside," she says with an eye roll.

"We'll figure something out. It's nearly Halloween, and the humans are on high alert from what I've heard."

Her mouth pops open, and her eyes light up. "I've always wanted to dress up for Halloween. It looks like so much fun."

"I can try to find you a mask to wear, but most of the time it draws more attention to your eyes."

"Can you find me a veil? It blocks people from being able to look directly into my eyes, and I can still see with it on."

"You know, that's a great idea. Let me get dressed, and I'll see if I can find one in town. Your clothes are here on the bed—probably underneath me, honestly." I say, giving her a quick kiss before I climb out of bed.

Chapter Ten

When Avyanna leaves for town, I get dressed and look around her apartment. There's really nothing to it. With her being a hunter, it makes sense. She travels a lot for work, and there's only so much she can travel with, especially if she's trying to get somewhere quickly. I can't help but wonder if the hunters have some sort of moving agency on speed dial or something of the sort.

I roll my eyes at the stupid thought. What does it matter if they have a moving agency? Avyanna can literally become other people; I'm sure she's able to get new stuff without needing money.

I'm just so used to my father, who could basically snap his fingers to get anything he wanted. I swear he had more money than I could ever comprehend, and he made sure everyone knew it when he was alive, too. For as long as I can remember, my father moved us from house to house, all over the world, each one furnished to the nines. I never knew whether he owned the homes we stayed in. Every time I tried to ask, he told me it wasn't my place. He also made it very clear that none of his assets would come to me when he died. It wasn't like I could argue with him because the only ones who knew I existed were the guards who used to protect me.

Since I was a little girl, I've longed for a family and to feel like I belong somewhere. Being locked up inside house after house, I gave up on that dream. Now that Avyanna has gotten me away from the guards who kept me under lock and key, maybe I can finally be happy. I know it's going to be difficult to integrate into society with my inability to look at people, but I want to make it work; I'm tired of being confined to one place.

The soft click of a door echoes down the hall, and I go on the defensive. Part of me hopes it's Avyanna, but if she's already back, I'll be shocked; she wasn't gone for long. However, I keep having to remind myself that we're far from any of the shops. I just didn't think it'd be easy to find a veil.

Heading toward the living room, I go to round the corner and run smack dab into Avyanna. I nearly fall, but she catches me, a smile cresting her lips.

"Going somewhere?" she asks nonchalantly.

"I *was* going to see if you were already back or if I was going to have to turn someone to stone for coming in here. Thankfully, it was the former and not the latter."

Her smile widens. "It's almost Halloween. Costumes are in every store that can get their hands on them. So, in light of that, I got you a full costume since you said you've always wanted to dress up."

Tears well in my eyes as I stare at her. My breath catches in my lungs when she pulls a beautiful black dress and a corresponding black veil out of a bag. No one has ever done something so nice for me.

Her eyes lock onto mine, and she drops everything she holds to wrap me up in her arms. "What's wrong, my little relic?"

I sniffle. "That was just so sweet of you."

She rubs her hand in circles on my back and chuckles. "Well, you did give me an amazing orgasm before I left. It gave me a little bit of a pep in my step, if you know what I mean."

Pushing away from her, I roll my eyes. "Is that all I need to do to get anything I want from you?"

"Maybe," she says, rolling her bottom lip between her teeth and staring at me with hooded eyes. "Why don't you go change before I decide to take you back to the bed and have my fill of you?"

My clit starts pulsing, and I curse under my breath. Her nostrils flare, a sign I'm learning means she smells my arousal, so I rush to pick up the bag of things she brought me and hurry to change.

After I squeeze into the form-fitting dress Avyanna bought—somehow perfectly knowing my size—I head into the bathroom to don the veil. As soon as I spot myself in the mirror, my jaw drops to the floor. I've never worn a dress like this. The beautiful silk hugs all my curves perfectly, although the dress is relatively short compared to the ones I'm accustomed to, barely reaching mid-thigh on me. The neckline is another thing altogether, plunging down to show off my usually nonexistent cleavage with lace adorning the cups in intricate designs.

Avyanna's silhouette coming up behind me in the mirror has me refocusing my attention. Her brows furrow as she gets closer. "Everything okay?"

I roll my shoulders back and step closer to the mirror to put my veil on. "Yep. All good."

Her lips purse, meeting my gaze in the mirror. Heat blossoms low in my belly, making me want to flee. How am I already so infatuated with her?

She clears her throat, and I realize I was staring at her lips. "What's going on in that pretty little head of yours?"

I gnaw on my lip. "I've never worn a dress like this, and... I really like it. Thank you."

The corner of her lips tips up into a small smile, and she comes to stand directly behind me. Placing her hands on my hips, she pulls me flush to her. I whimper, loving having her so close.

I watch in the mirror as she places a gentle kiss on my neck and then sucks my earlobe into her mouth, nibbling on it lightly. My knees grow weak, making me nearly fall to the floor.

She tuts and wraps her arms around me to keep me standing. "My, my. You're so easy to tease."

"It seems like my body is at your beck and call," I say with a sultry undertone to my voice.

Her tongue darts out to lick a trail up my neck to my ear. "I do owe you an orgasm."

I shake my head and sigh. "Not now. We should get to my father's house sooner rather than later. The longer we wait, the more guards they'll be pulling in to look for me. I'd rather not fight with the lot of them unless I have to."

With one last kiss to my neck, she huffs out a grunt. "Fine. Let's get this over with."

Pulling out of her hold, I adjust my veil. Avyanna continues to stand behind me, looking me up and down. Her ice-blue eyes darken, making it hard for me not to turn around and crush my lips to hers.

But then I realize what she's wearing. Since I've come into the bathroom, she's changed into a sleek black tuxedo with a slim green tie, one that matches the color of my eyes perfectly. My heart flutters hard in my chest, a feeling that's both unfamiliar and not entirely unpleasant.

Avyanna chuckles, pulling me out of my trance. "If you're going to just stare at me, I'm going to have a hard time not ripping that dress off you. Aren't we supposed to be getting out of here?"

I clear my throat and mutter a quick 'brat' before finishing my attempt to get myself ready.

Chapter Eleven

Vaelyn

When I wake up the morning after our night together, Adrestia is still fast asleep. She's wrapped her arm around my waist, and I'm conflicted about how I should feel. I love the way it feels, but at the same time, I want to run—to get away before things get too real. Even though this is something I've always wanted, things feel like they're moving too fast.

I watch her sleep for a moment because she just looks so peaceful. Then, I slip out from under her arm to search for my clothes, which are strewn across the floor. After watching TV and movies last night, we couldn't keep our hands off each other, and that's how we ended up in her bed again. When we'd both had a couple of orgasms each, we drifted off to sleep. I didn't intend to stay the night with her, but it happened anyway.

Once I'm dressed again, I find a piece of paper and a pen in the kitchen so I can scribble out a quick note before I leave. I don't want her to panic, but I need to think for a bit—without her clouding my judgement. When I'm in her presence, all I want is to stay with her. That's never happened to me before.

I slip out onto the balcony and shift into my harpy form. Being like this makes me feel incredibly free. As I approach the railing, my eyes drift over the city. There's something deep inside me that wants to go down there, to explore the streets and everything this place has to offer.

It's strange for me to be drawn to a place like this. I normally avoid big cities because they remind me too much of home—somewhere I never intend to return. But the longer I stand here, the harder it becomes to avoid the desire to look around.

With it being daylight, I'll have to be careful to keep myself out of sight. Usually, I hide within the clouds, and if there aren't any, I fly as high as I can, so I look like any other bird. The problem right now is that if I fly too far outside the city, I'll have further to walk back into the city limits. However, if I land in the trees nearby, someone could see me. That would be a disaster in itself. Too bad there isn't really a happy medium.

I launch off the balcony without another thought and begin my ascent. Once I'm high enough above the city, I reassess my options. It's still early enough in the day, and it's the weekend, so there isn't much going on yet. Everyone is saving up their energy for Halloween in a few days, which just so happens to be one of my favorite holidays. I love seeing how humans imagine us supernaturals and all the other crazy things they come up with. Some of the little kids also look freaking adorable dressed up.

With the fact that I see only a few cars on the streets so far, I decide it's safe enough for me to land in the woods on the outskirts of the city. I'll still keep an eye out for pedestrians and whatnot, but I should be fine.

I fly just above the trees and look around again for anyone who could spot me. Thankfully, no one is there, so I swoop down and shift into my human form quickly. My eyes drift around, still concerned someone is around me. Let's just say that being discovered by humans has always been one of my biggest fears. When I'm absolutely certain no one is nearby, I adjust my clothes and wander out of the trees.

The first thing that greets me is a series of small-business storefronts. The one that catches my eye immediately is a bookstore boasting its selection of new and used books. It looks like the store itself was once an old greenhouse repurposed as a shop. Clear windows bubble out from the building, showing off rows of books both inside and out. I'm itching to go inside, but I know that if I do, I'll want something, and I don't have any money at the moment.

One thing I refuse to do is steal from small businesses. They already work so hard to stay afloat. Big-name companies are another story in my book. They can afford to lose a few items here and there, so I don't feel as bad about stealing from them when I need to. At least being on the move means I don't need as much.

Reluctantly, I continue down the street, looking over all the shops. While all the shops are adorable, nothing else truly catches my eye, so I continue down the street. I mindlessly pass building after building, letting my feet carry me wherever they please. Jack-o'-lanterns litter every doorstep, even trickling onto the sidewalks in places, because there are just so many of them. Part of me likes to think that means the area is full of big, happy families.

As I walk, I admire the mix of old and new buildings, which is quite unusual for a city of its size. One side of the town has older brick buildings with windows in perfect rows and columns. The other side has newer buildings, primarily constructed from metal with massive windows that fill the majority of the walls, much like Adrestia's penthouse.

And then there are the mansions on the outskirts of the city, which are fucking stunning. I've never seen anything like them up close, but I guess that's the thing about avoiding places like this—I've missed out on a lot of the unique infrastructure that big cities have to offer.

Truthfully, anything is better than what I saw while I was in the nest.

Circling back, I head toward the city center, where there's a massive park with a gorgeous marble water fountain in the center. I'm just down the street, stuck in my thoughts, when I trip on one of the jack-o'-lanterns that rolled onto the sidewalk. I try to catch myself, but there's nothing for me to grab onto, so I prepare to hit the ground.

But I don't. Instead, I land face-first in the chest of an unsuspecting woman. When her arms wrap around my body to steady me, I right myself and scramble back.

"I-I'm so sorry," I say, but then pause when I look at the woman. She's wearing a tight-fitting black dress with an uncharacteristically thick black veil covering her face. Through it, I still catch a glimpse of her vibrant, slitted, emerald-green eyes.

Jumping back, I gasp, but another woman is behind me before I can make any other movements. "Interesting. Someone else who doesn't turn to stone by looking at you, Roxi."

Roxi's eyes flick to the other woman. "My veil is covering my eyes."

My brows slam down. "What the fuck is that supposed to mean?"

The woman behind me snickers. "You just looked a gorgon straight in the eyes. And you're not a statue now."

I stare wide-eyed at the woman before me, her eyes now focused on her feet. "Like she said, she has a veil on that's covering her eyes, so if she is a gorgon—which I'm fairly sure she isn't because they're extinct—that's impeding it from happening."

Another laugh rumbles at my back as the woman leans in and sniffs me. "Is that a challenge, little bird?"

"You guys are insane, and I'm leaving now," I say, trying to step away.

A hand wraps around my bicep, and I swing my other arm back to elbow her, but she grabs that, too. Then she's pulling me backward, to I don't even know where. The supposed gorgon follows us, making sure to avoid eye contact with me.

I'm fighting to get away, but the woman behind me tsks. "The more you fight, the harder this will be on you."

"Where are you taking me?" I demand through gritted teeth.

"Away from prying eyes so we can talk for a moment," she whispers in my ear.

"Let me go and I'll happily fucking walk," I hiss.

Now, both of them are laughing. The supposed gorgon finally speaks, "We all know you're going to try to run if she lets you go."

"More like fly," the woman holding me says.

"So that's why you called her little bird. Makes sense," the gorgon says with a shrug.

I huff out a breath and let them lead me to an alleyway. The woman behind me shoves me against the wall. When she finally comes around to where I can see her, I look her over. She stands at least half a foot taller than me, and the sleek tux she's wearing hides her build well, which should be intimidating considering how easily she hauled my ass back here, but it's not. Most adults, both human and supernatural, are taller than me, plus I know how to hold my own, as I easily showed Adrestia last night.

My gaze reaches her face, and I freeze. I know exactly who this is. Her lips turn up in a smirk, like she knows that something has clicked into place for me, and her gorgeous ice-blue eyes turn pure black. My heart feels like it's going to beat out of my chest. A hunter, especially one of Avyanna's status, confronting you like this is never a good sign.

"Are you here for me?" I ask, scared to hear the answer.

Avyanna shakes her head. "I'm intrigued by the fact you could look Roxi here in the eye and not turn to stone."

"She had a veil over her eyes, and gorgons are extinct," I say with a scoff.

Roxi rolls her eyes and rips her veil off her head. In the next second, a shimmer creeps across her skin, and I come face to face with a gorgon in the flesh. My jaw drops to the floor. I can't look away from her, even though everything logical in me screams that this is a guaranteed death if I don't.

Her voice is deep yet melodic when she speaks in this form. "We're clearly not completely extinct, seeing as I'm alive and all."

Our eyes meet and hold there for a moment before she looks away. A shimmer returns her to her human form shortly after. I'm still awestruck. And, amazed, nothing has happened to me.

Avyanna's hollow laugh pulls me out of my trance. "It didn't happen in that form either. Interesting. You're coming with us."

My head whips in her direction. "Excuse me?"

"I think you heard me just fine," Avyanna growls.

A tall figure stomps into the alleyway and shoves Avyanna up against the wall opposite me. "Like fuck she is."

Chapter Twelve

ADRESTIA

When I woke up and found Vaelyn gone, disappointment flooded through me. I really thought we had something, but maybe I was wrong. Or, I was hopeful she would give me a chance.

Then, I found her note in the kitchen, and disappointment turned to anger.

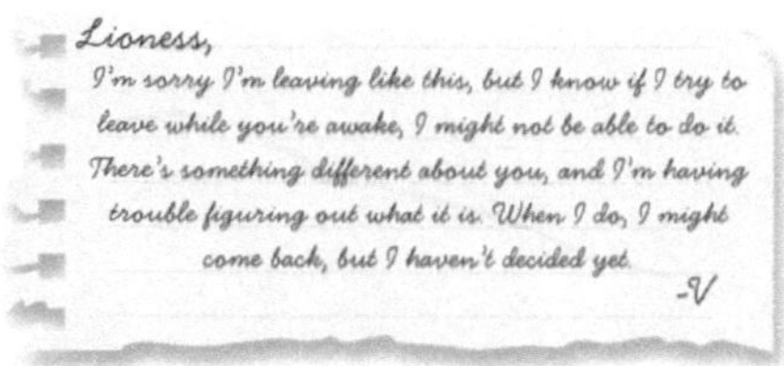

After I found the note, I tried to distract myself by getting ready and working on the case. When I saw the agents from S.I.R.E.N. the night before, I clarified that they still had the other bodies. I'd seen them at the scenes since I was the first responding agent, but I needed to look at them again, so their headquarters was my first stop this morning.

When I get there, they already have the three bodies laid out for me on slabs in the freezer. All three are human women with dark, wavy hair and pale, unmarked skin. None of them are tall per se, but they're all curvy. I would say our perpetrator has a type.

Going from woman to woman, I compare their injuries. With the first, the perp was messy as all get out, making me think it was his first time. She has claw marks across her face and legs, but then the perp tore through her abdomen, ripping through some of her organs. There was a lot of blood at this scene, so I'm sure it was all over the perp.

With the second victim, our perp was a lot more methodical. Claw marks are still across her face, but I think they got this one to go into the courtyard willingly, unlike the first one, because when S.I.R.E.N. did her rape kit, it came back positive for sperm. Upon further examination, they discovered that she'd recently had sex; however, we weren't sure whether it was consensual or not. Either way, her injuries weren't as frenzied, but they were still deadly. Instead of ripping her open, the perp bit into her, eating her as if she were some sort of sandwich.

The third victim's attack seemed to have started similarly to the second: she'd recently had sex; there was semen still in her vaginal canal when we found her; claw marks streak across her face; and the perp bit into her. However, with this victim, he was interrupted. Barely any of her body was missing when we found her.

With each attack, the perp has seemed to hone his abilities. The thing I can't get over is that they're eating their victims. But why? It's too bad I can't ask Avyanna. She'd have a better insight into the monster I'm looking for.

On my way back home to look into monsters that eat flesh, two very familiar scents hit me—Avyanna *and* Vaelyn. What are they doing together? How on earth would they even know each other? I follow their scents to an alleyway where I find Vaelyn up against a wall with Avyanna standing before her and a... gorgon?

What in the actual fuck is going on here?

Then I hear Avyanna tell Vaelyn that she's taking Vaelyn with her, and I lose my shit. I stomp into the alley, grab Avyanna by the throat, and shove her against the wall. "Like fuck she is."

Avyanna's eyes widen, but I don't let up until Vaelyn has her hand on my arm, trying to rip me away from my mimic. "Adrestia, what the hell are you doing? She's a fucking hunter!"

"I know exactly who she is," I growl. "I also know that she can absolutely kick my ass if she really wants to."

Hissing sounds come from my left just before a voice I haven't heard yet speaks. "Let her go."

My gaze flicks to the gorgon before I think better of it. I immediately avert my gaze and wait for my body to begin turning to stone. When it doesn't happen, Avyanna taps my arm. I let her drop to the ground and step back until I hit the wall where Vaelyn had just been.

"You didn't turn to stone either," Avyanna says with a raspy voice. Then, she's in front of me, hand on my chin, making me look at her. "Listen to me. I want you to look her dead in the eye again."

My eyes widen. "Are you out of your mind?"

"Maybe a little," she says with a hint of a smile. "But you didn't turn to stone with that look, and if her look had affected you, you absolutely should've. I don't think you are, though. I'm not, and neither is our harpy friend here. Please, just look her in the eye again. Prove me right."

"I'm not ready to die," I whisper, tears filling my eyes.

Avyanna runs her thumb over my bottom lip. "You're not going to die, Addie."

Hearing her call me that after so long does something to me. A tear rolls down my cheek, and I take a deep breath before my eyes drift to the gorgon. She's already staring at me with her jaw clenched and her snakes hissing. I'm guessing something about this interaction between Avie and me is upsetting her, but I still look her in the eye and prepare for the worst.

Her eyes shimmer like the most exquisite emeralds I've ever seen, making it impossible to look away. I almost want to get lost in them. But then she looks away from me, and Avyanna pulls away from me in the next second, walking to where the gorgon still stands. Vaelyn stands against the opposite wall, mouth agape, and face even paler than it was previously.

I walk over to where she stands and cup her face in my hands, crashing my lips to hers in a desperate kiss. She lets me kiss her for a few seconds before she shoves me away. When she tries to leave, I grab her arm and pull her back to me.

"I can't do this right now," she says.

"Don't leave yet," I plead.

Her gaze turns severe. "I saw the way you looked at her, Adrestia. She means something to you, and I can't get in the middle of that when I'm still trying to figure out what I feel for you."

"Look, I had something with Avyanna a long time ago, and she wants nothing to do with me anymore. So, while I may still have feelings for her, it's not going anywhere."

Vaelyn rolls her eyes. "The way she spoke to you says something totally different."

"She just wanted me to listen to her, and she knows how to get what she wants from me."

"Whatever. Deny it all you want."

My jaw clenches. "Please stay. You've been a drifter for far too long, and I can give you somewhere to call home again."

Her eyes fill with tears, and she rips her arm from my grasp. "Fuck. You. Adrestia. We fucked and spent one night together. You don't know anything about me or what I need."

"I may not, but I want to—I want *you*. While that might sound a little crazy because we only met yesterday, I'm drawn to you like a moth to a flame. I know that's really fucking cliché, but I don't want to let you go. Last night was one of the most incredible nights of my fucking life, and that wasn't just because of the sex. It was your being there, talking to me, and keeping me company."

Vaelyn's nostrils flare as she huffs out a breath. "Last night was nothing."

"You're a fucking liar, and you know it!" I hiss.

"Goodbye, Adrestia. Have a nice life," she says flatly, although her eyes tell me a different story as they glisten.

"No," I growl. "Don't do this. Stay. Let's figure this out together. If it turns out to be nothing, then you can go, and I won't stop you."

But she doesn't stop her trek out of the alley.

Chapter Thirteen

There's too much going on today, and I can't handle it anymore. I put my veil back on as I start walking down the alley. Avyanna catches up to me, hurrying around me to block my path, but I skirt around her. She appears in front of me again and stops me this time, so I turn around, trying to go back down the alley, but she's in front of me in the blink of an eye.

Her hands grab onto my shoulders to keep me in place, but my gorgon form takes over, and my snakes start hissing at her. "Let me go, Avyanna."

She shakes her head. "Where the hell do you think you're going?"

"Away from here. I don't know what I was thinking when I allowed you to take me to your place. I was so desperate to get away from my father's house that I didn't stop to question what I was doing."

Her brows furrow. "What's that supposed to mean?"

"I wanted you to be my knight in shining armor; I wanted so badly for you to swoop in and take care of me when no one else would. It was too good to be true, though—there's something between you and... Addie? I don't even fucking know at this point. I've been living in my dreams, apparently, thinking you would just be the perfect person right off the bat."

She huffs out a laugh. "First off, Adrestia and I have nothing going on now. She's one of my exes. Because of something that happened between us, I don't want her or anything she has to offer anymore—"

"That's bullshit, and you know it."

"It's not. I want you, not her."

I roll my eyes. "It's possible you want her *and* me, but I'm not getting in the middle of that shit right now. Especially if there's this level of tension. You need to figure that shit out. I don't know any of the details, nor do I need to, but you need to work it out for yourself," I say, taking a step back. "Look, I've got some shit to figure out. I've looked three supes in the eye and not had any of them turn into stone, so I wonder if it's a me thing at this point. Maybe I'm fucking broken. Or maybe I don't even turn others to stone like I've been told."

"There's nothing wrong with you, Roxi," she says, trying to reach for me.

I take another step back, feeling defeated. "I just need to go home for a bit."

"They're going to move you if you go back, and you know I will track you down again."

"I'm not going anywhere unless I want to this time."

Her hands go up in surrender. "Fine. Go then. I'll give you a little space, but I won't be far if you need me."

"I'm a big girl. I can handle myself."

Separating myself from Avyanna when I did was a stupid idea. I have no clue where I am or where I'm going. It wasn't like I'd gotten to wander around at any point when we left her apartment. Hell, I've never been able to leave the fucking house except when we moved.

I walk in the direction I think I need to go, keeping my eyes on the ground in case I accidentally make eye contact and can actually turn someone to stone.

When I reach the edge of downtown, I glance around. A man stands down the street, looking at me like I'm the strangest person he's ever seen, and I decide to chance it.

Walking up to him, I say, "Excuse me, sir. I'm a little lost. Can you tell me where I might find Cherry Street?"

"Uh, sure. It's a few blocks north," he says, pointing in the direction I assume is north. Then he looks me over and asks. "Are you okay?"

I give him a small smile while still looking at the ground. "Yes, I am. I apologize. I have a very hard time with eye contact. Thank you for your help."

With that, I walk past him and continue in the direction he pointed. Three blocks later, I come across Cherry Street. Thankfully, I remember the address of the most recent home I occupied: 5280 Cherry Street. The house on the corner I'm at is 1401. Looking in one direction, I notice the numbers seem to increase, while in the other direction, the numbers decrease.

Looks like I've got a way to walk.

I get started, and I walk for what seems like forever before a van pulls up beside me. A man jumps out with a canvas bag in hand, running straight for me. I start to run, but he's too fast. He throws the bag over my head and pulls me back against him so he can wrap something around my wrists. I struggle, but he hauls me back until I'm thrown onto a cold metal surface, which I assume is the van's floor. Doors slam behind me, and then we're off.

We don't drive for long before the door is yanked open again, and I'm thrown over someone's shoulder. I kick and thrash in the person's arms, but they just laugh at my attempts.

"You aren't going anywhere, precious curse. Daddy instructed us to keep a good eye on you, even after he died, and that's what we plan on doing. After what happened with Merric, though, we plan to have a little fun with you," a seductive male voice says.

I stop thrashing. "You wouldn't fucking dare touch me without my permission."

Several men chuckle around me, but the same man speaks again. "Who said we need your permission? You can't do anything with this bag over your head. You won't even know who's touching you, so you can't send someone after us either."

My jaw clenches so hard I'm amazed I don't shatter my teeth. "I will force every single one of you to look into my eyes and turn each of you to stone."

A man tuts before a new man speaks. "See, one of us heard you've been looking at other supes and not turning them to stone, so I'm not sure it's going to matter either way."

"We'll see about that," I hiss.

The man carrying me begins walking up some stairs, and the scent of blood hits me. It's overly harsh, unlike anything I've ever smelled, making me want to puke. When we reach level ground again, the scent hits me harder, and I start to gag.

"Aww. Is demon blood too much for you? The hunter must have ripped into him after you took off, so you weren't exposed to it. We'll get it cleaned up soon," the man carrying me says.

I bring my foot down, trying to kick him, but he catches it with his free hand. "Put me down. I feel like I'm going to throw up," I say.

The first man who spoke to me scoffs. "Take her to the other room. I'm not about to take that hood off right now. I want to have my fun before she tries to kill me."

We pass the worst of the smell, and I try to breathe through my mouth so I don't vomit. My stomach is nearly settled when I'm thrown onto a soft surface that feels a lot like a bed, stealing the wind from my lungs. In the next moment, I plant my feet against the surface and try to push myself away from the man who threw me down.

I'm not fast enough. Hands wrap around my ankles tightly and pull me until my ass is barely on the bed. I try to sit up, but another set of hands grabs my bound wrists, pulling them above my head.

My eyes fill with tears as I thrash against their hold. "Please don't do this."

One of the men crawls onto the bed beside me and tsks. "We haven't even gotten started, sweetheart. Now, lie still so we can get this dress off you. I love how tight it is—showing off all those beautiful curves—but I want full access to your body. We're going to mark you up so fucking pretty."

A sob racks through me just as something slices through the material of my dress. A sharp pain slices across my bare breast, and someone hums in appreciation. Then, a tongue is licking up the blood trickling from the wound.

"Fear always makes blood taste sweeter," the man who carried me says from near my breast.

One of the other men agrees as a tongue licks up from my breast to my neck. Then, that person bites down, fangs piercing the skin above my carotid artery. My back arches, and I go to scream, but a hand clamps over my mouth before I can get any sound out.

Tears stream down my cheeks because I know there's nothing I can do now—so much for being able to handle my own. The fangs in my neck retract, and the man growls as he sucks at my neck.

"Don't take too much. We can't have her dying now, can we?" the man at my feet snaps, moving his hands up my legs to spread my thighs.

The man at my neck growls and releases his suction. Then he licks the puncture wounds before pushing away from me. "Get on with it. I want my fucking turn."

"I'll do it when I'm damn well and ready. You already got to taste her," the man at my feet says.

The sound of a zipper near my center has me fighting again, loosening the hand on my mouth. But hands clamp down on my thighs, and the man at my feet hisses, "Stop fucking moving. You're only making this that much harder on yourself. We're going to make you feel real good, so just lie back and relax, precious curse."

My chest shakes as I cry harder. I'm not sure I'm going to get out of this. I just know that if I don't, they're going to kill me. Emotion clogs my throat as I plead for them to stop again.

The hands on my thighs move to lift my legs and pull me further down. My ass is now hanging off the edge, only being held up by the man holding my lower half hostage. His hard length nudges against my entrance, and I whimper, just wanting him to stop.

Another sharp sting cuts across my breast, distracting me momentarily from the man entering me in one swift thrust. My back bows off the bed, and I scream. I'm not wet in the least, so his thrusts hurt, making me feel like he's ripping me apart.

The pressure on my wrists shifts as one hand takes them both. A hand, likely from the man above me, starts to cover my mouth, which makes the man raping me stop. "Don't. I want to hear her scream while I fuck her tight cunt."

"Fine. Just as long as we don't attract any unwanted attention," the man above me says.

My screams continue until the man fucking me comes inside me with a grunt. After he comes down off his high, he collapses on top of me and kisses my neck. "We'll work on getting you wetter next time."

Then he's gone, and someone else replaces him. I try to kick at them, but they grab my calves tightly and tsk.

"That wasn't very nice," the man who bit me says.

"I don't fucking care! Don't touch me!" I scream.

"I'm going to have this pussy whether you want me to or not," he says, nestling into my sore center.

"Just stop. Please fucking stop," I beg, even though I know it's not going to help my case.

His cock twitches against me. "You sound so pretty when you beg."

"Go fuck yourself, you piece of shit. I bet you can't even get it up unless you're taking something that doesn't belong to you," I hiss.

He thrusts himself into me so hard the bed bangs against the wall. Then his hands come down on either side of me. "Don't speak about something you know nothing about." *thrust* "You should also be careful poking this bear." *thrust* "My fuse is pretty short." *thrust* "And I'll rip you to shreds if you're not careful."

I sniffle. "I don't fucking care. Just get this over with and kill me already."

The man holding my hands laughs. "We're not going to kill you, little gorgon. You're our plaything now."

Chapter Fourteen

Vaelyn

I don't know where the hell I'm going, but I don't want to leave the city yet. For some reason, I want to accept Adrestia's offer, even though I know I shouldn't. There's clearly still something going on between her and the hunter. Adrestia can deny it all she wants, but the way the hunter regarded her—spoke to her, and touched her—was full of love and longing. I have no qualms about polyamory; I just can't be in the middle of a tense situation like that, so they'll have to figure shit out before I even think about a relationship with Adrestia.

My mindless walking leads me into the beautiful neighborhood with the mansions I saw earlier. I admire the houses for a bit until a woman's scream pierces the air, pulling my attention back to reality. Someone is in trouble, and I need to help them.

Not completely sure where I'm going, my body moves of its own volition, rushing to get to the screaming woman, and I'm in front of the mansion where the screams are emanating from faster than I thought possible for my body. Another scream pierces the air, and I rush toward the door. When I try to open it, I find that it's locked. Cursing under my breath, I hurry to the back of the house and find a sliding glass door that's been haphazardly left open. I thank my lucky stars for this one break, squeezing through the gap so I don't draw attention to myself.

The woman screams again, the sound coming from upstairs, and begs for someone to stop. My mind jumps to the worst-case scenario—she's being tortured or raped. I rush to find the stairs, and when I do, I go up them as fast as I can without making too much noise. A man grunting fills the hall just as the woman's sobs intensify.

Now I'm seeing red. I take slow, calculated steps down the hall, straining my ears to hear everything I can.

"Last but not least," a gruff voice says.

"No, please, no more," the woman cries. Her voice sounds familiar, but I can't recall where I've heard it before.

A man laughs, and another deep voice says, "Last one, precious curse. You're doing so fucking well. How I wish I could lick up those beautiful tears, though."

"When I find out who you are, I'm going to kill you," the woman says, venom dripping from every word.

I stop just outside the door where the voices are coming from. It's cracked just enough for me to peek inside, and I watch as a man, naked from the waist down, thrusts into a nude woman. She lies completely bare before him, her hands tied and held by another man positioned above her head.

Her scream pierces the air, and before I can stop myself, I'm shoving the door open. I rip the man raping her away and throw him to the ground. Fury courses through my blood as I approach him. But he transforms before me, a black shadow taking over to make him larger than he'd been.

A demon.

Which I've never dealt with before.

The door behind me is thrown open again, slamming hard against the wall, and all I see is a blur of movement entering the room. A woman stops before the demon at my feet, the visible bits of her skin literally rippling like water. She reaches directly into the center of the demon's shadowy depths, pulling out something that glows an odd green from the area where his chest should be.

His body slackens—he's already dead.

Across the room, another man I hadn't noticed whispers, "Oh, fuck."

He moves just as fast as the black-haired woman beside me, but she's catching up to him in an instant, jumping onto his back, and sinking her teeth into his neck. Reaching over his head, he grabs her hair and then stumbles, knees hitting the floor, although he recovers quickly, jumping back to his feet. As he does this, one of the woman's hands digs into his shoulder while the other wraps around his throat. The man screams, but it turns into a gurgle when the woman rips out his trachea, and he falls face-first onto the floor. The woman jumps off before she joins him. Blood streams down her chin onto her clothes, and I finally realize who she is.

The hunter—Avyanna.

Her eyes are pure black as they meet mine. "Find her some clothes or a blanket. Quickly."

My eyes dart around the room, taking in my surroundings for the first time since I entered, while Avyanna takes off toward the remaining man, who's just staring at us in shock. The woman on the bed lies there limp. I have the urge to check on her, but I know

Avyanna will do so when she takes care of the last threat.

I return my attention to looking around the room. Just beyond where Avyanna downed the second man, I spot what looks to be a walk-in closet. I don't pay the dead man any attention as I step over him and begin my search for something to wrap the woman in. Numerous blankets sit nicely folded on a shelf, so I grab a couple of them and head back into the room.

As I walk through the doorway, the last man screams. Avyanna has him on his knees, her hand in his hair, forcing him to look up at her.

He begs, "Please. I was just doing what they told me to do. They threatened my family."

Avyanna's voice resonates through the room as she gets in his face. "Your family is already dead, Lyall. I know everything there is to know about you. I know everything about all the men who were tasked with watching over her. And still you failed because you're a pathetic excuse of a man. I can see right through you. I know what you've done, and I know you enjoyed touching what is *mine*. My only wish is that I had more time to make you suffer."

The man starts begging again, but Avyanna snaps his neck, the sound echoing through the room. She lets his body fall to the floor and returns to the woman on the bed, who lies eerily still. I approach, holding my breath as Avyanna removes the cloth sack from the woman's head.

It's Roxi.

Avyanna checks Roxi over, her skin doing the weird rippling thing the closer she looks. Bruises already dot Roxi's ankles, hips, and wrists, but some have started to develop on other parts of her body. What the hell did they do to the poor woman?

Ripping a blanket from my hand, Avyanna says, "I need to get her to my apartment. She can't be here anymore. I'm not letting her out of my sight again. Ever."

"It's not your fau—"

After laying the blanket over Roxi, Avyanna rounds back on me. "It *is* my fault! I didn't make sure she got home safely. I was frustrated about what happened in the alley, so I tried to walk it off. But I felt deep down that something was wrong, and I came straight here. When I heard her screaming, I lost it. I should've kept at least one of them alive so I could question them. Fuck!"

Her hand runs through her hair, and I'm itching to try to calm her down. "It was her choice to leave you in the alley. You were just trying to give her some space. What matters most now is that you're here."

"You're right, but I don't feel any better about it. I knew I should've followed her until she was safe."

"The past is in the past. Let's leave it there. We can't change what happened, but we can definitely influence what will happen next," I say.

She paces back and forth in front of Roxi. Then she stops abruptly and turns to where Roxi lies. "How did they even know where she was?"

"Could they have been following her?" I ask.

"If they have, they probably know where I live," she says, mumbling some quiet curses under her breath. "I'm going to have to find somewhere else for us to stay. They won't ever lay another hand on her."

I bite my lip. "Adrestia has a penthouse in town. I can take you there for now."

Avyanna rolls her eyes. "Adrestia is one of the reasons Roxi took off in the first place, so I'm not sure that would be a great idea."

I scoff. "Well, you're the biggest reason I took off."

"Me? Why?"

"Because of the way you look at Adrestia, and the way she seems to revere you. I'm not sure what happened exactly between you guys, but I know you still have feelings for each other, and I can't get in the middle of that right now," I say, staring at the floor.

Avyanna approaches me. "Adrestia and I were together a long time ago, and her family stuck their noses where they didn't belong. She didn't stop them, and things quickly went south. I have no interest in letting that ever happen to me again, so while I may still have feelings for her I don't want to admit, a relationship between us will never happen again."

"Never say never, Avyanna," I mutter.

She gives me a sad smile, her ice-blue eyes reflecting the depth of her emotions warring inside her.

Chapter Fifteen

Avyanna

Looking into Vaelyn's stormy grey eyes like this, I feel something else I haven't felt in a long, long time—intrigue and desire. I don't understand it. Could it be because I smell Adrestia on her? Am I still drawn to Adrestia as much as I was all those years ago?

What I told Vaelyn about Adrestia was the truth; we likely couldn't have a functioning relationship after what happened. I'm not sure I could trust her again, even if I wanted to. But then Alaric's claims come back to me: *You really think she just stood by and let them do as they pleased with you without interfering? How the hell do you think you were able to get out?*

Maybe it's time I finally talked to Adrestia about what happened.

"I'll take Roxi to Adrestia's under one condition," I say.

She raises an eyebrow. "And what would that be?"

I take a deep breath. "You go with us."

She crosses her arms over her chest and stares into my eyes. "Fine."

"Just 'fine'? No argument?"

"I have nothing better to do right now. And I'd like to make sure she's okay," she says, nodding toward Roxi.

"That's understandable. Thank you."

"You don't need to thank me. They really did a number on her."

I take a deep breath to keep myself from losing it again. "Are you able to fly with Roxi in your arms?"

She nods. "My wings aren't attached to my arms."

"Good. I need you to take her for me, please. It'll look really strange if I waltzed into Adrestia's apartment building carrying an unconscious, naked woman."

"That'd be interesting to witness. At least she's wrapped in blankets," Vaelyn says, holding back a laugh. "So, I take it you can't fly?"

I shake my head. "I wasn't graced with that ability. I have tried to change into several flying supes, but I'm not able to get the wings to work."

"Interesting, but unfortunate. I can carry her with no problem, but I won't be able to carry you at the same time. So I can fly you there one at a time, or you can head there on foot by yourself. The only problem with that is that I don't know the address or how to get there from the ground. If you could fly, it would be a totally different story, and you could follow me."

"It's fine. What do you remember about the surrounding area?"

She shrugs. "Not much. I didn't really have a chance to look around while I was on her balcony. I did notice that her building was the tallest in the city."

"She must live in the Luxur building," I say confidently, even though I feel everything but that at the moment. "It was the first building that drew my attention when I got here."

"Then you know how to get there, I assume?" I nod and she continues, "Great. If you're not there in thirty minutes, one of us will come looking for you."

My eyes drop to the beautiful gorgon on the bed. Not much of her pale skin is visible with the blanket covering her, but bruises cover every bit that is. If I hadn't already killed the disgusting men around me, I would track them down one by one and torture them.

I lean down, kissing Roxi's forehead before I turn to Vaelyn. "I'll see you guys there. Please, just... be careful."

Vaelyn walks up to me and places her hands on my arms. "We'll be fine. The building really isn't far from here, and flying supes in the city tend to be pretty rare as it is."

I let out a sigh and drop my head in defeat. Vaelyn catches me off guard when she rises onto the tips of her toes to gently kiss my cheek.

Before I can say anything, she's pulled away and scooped Roxi up to head out the door. I stand there in shock, listening to her footsteps echo down the hall as she descends the stairs. That was... unexpected.

When the shock finally wears off, I turn toward the door, and a blinding blue light flashes in the room.

Not again.

"Were we not just here yesterday?" Alaric asks behind me as the light dissipates.

"I tried to keep her away from here, but shit happened, and she decided to come back. Except before she got here, these three fuckers abducted her from the street and took advantage of her. They tied a fucking bag over her head so she couldn't look at them. There was no way I would allow them to get away with that," I hiss, rounding on him.

He holds a hand up, stopping me in my tracks. "Anna, stop. You will do well to remember that I am a friend, not a foe. I am not here to bring you in; I am here to take care of your mess. Again. This time, I will have to call in the others as well. There is not just a demon for me to take care of this time."

I let out a long breath and will my heart to slow. "I wouldn't make a mess if I didn't have to. Roxanna is covered in bruises, pretty much from head to toe, because of these pieces of shit. They deserved a hell of a lot worse than they got, but getting her to safety was my top priority."

He glances around the room. "If safety were your true priority, where is she?"

"Clearly no longer here."

"No shit, Sherlock," he grumbles.

"It's a long story, but I sent her with someone to Adrestia's place in the city."

That catches his attention. "You must be on speaking terms with her then?"

I roll my eyes. "Not exactly. We haven't discussed anything, but it's the safest place I could take Roxi for now."

"How do you think Roxanna will feel about you bringing her to Adrestia's?"

"She's already aware of my prior relationship with Adrestia. They actually met earlier, and that led to this whole situation."

His brows shoot to his hairline. "Do tell."

"I think not, Alaric. It's none of your business."

He pouts. "But I thought we were friends."

My eyes narrow on him. "Fine. It all started when this harpy literally ran into Roxi while we were on our way here. They looked each other in the eye without anything happening, and I dragged the harpy into an alley so we could talk more. Then Adrestia showed up and accidentally looked into Roxi's eyes, too. I let my emotions get the best of me when we figured that out, which upset both Roxi and the harpy." I finish my long-winded explanation, and he stares blankly at me. "If that's all you'd like to know, I really need—"

"She looked each of you in the eyes without conse-quence?" he asks with little emotion.

"Yeah… What is it?" I ask, suspicion creeping into my voice.

"Have you heard humans use the term soulmates?"

"Of course. They use it for everyone they feel they have some sort of connection with," I say with a scoff.

His eyes darken as they focus on me again. "They're very real in the supernatural world, Anna. Some species believe you can have more than one person you connect with on a spiritual level, just as humans do, but I agree they take it to another level."

I cross my arms over my chest. "What does this have to do with Roxi and all three of us being able to look into her eyes?"

"She's the first gorgon to have been born in cen-turies—"

"I'm well aware of that. I was alive when they were killed off. Hell, I even killed some of them myself," I say, getting irritated.

His eyes narrow at me. "Let me finish my explanation, Avyanna. Several eons ago, gorgons roamed the Earth in search of their Synkairós—Synkai for short. Their Synkai were like their soulmates, yet so much more. A life partner. Someone who understood them and didn't fear them. A missing piece of their soul. Without them, they were destined for insanity.

"From what I understand, gorgons weren't limited to one Synkai. The most impressive thing about this, though, is that gorgons and their Synkai could make eye contact without anything happening to either person. Sound familiar?"

My mouth hangs open. I'm completely speechless.

Alaric laughs. "Your kind have something like a soulmate they believe in, too, right?"

"We do. Sielunkumppani," I whisper.

He nods. "That's Finnish, right? Meaning soul companion?"

"Yeah. I was born and mostly raised in what's considered modern-day Finland, so Finnish was my first language. But I've never believed in Sielunkumppani before. I've never seen anyone who has one," I say, staring off into space.

"How many others of your kind do you actually know?"

"I haven't met another doppelgänger in centuries. Even before then, I'd only ever really seen my family."

A smile spreads across Alaric's face. "Exactly. So how would you even know if it's real or not, according to your kind's definition?"

"You're not wrong," I mumble, still staring into space.

"Could Adrestia and Roxanna possibly be this for you?"

My eyes drift to him again. "I have absolutely no clue."

"Do they make you feel like you belong with them?" Alaric asks.

I consider his question for a minute before replying. "They do. But how do you know that?"

He shrugs. "I've been around for a very long time, as have you. But we've worked on opposite sides of the coin. You know more about the monsters of the supernatural world—that's been your specialty for years. I know a little bit about a lot of things. Just because I'm 'The Retriever' for the demons does not mean that's all I know about."

"That kind of felt like an insult, but whatever. This is just a lot to comprehend," I say, ending on a whisper.

Alaric shakes his head. "It wasn't an insult in the least, Anna. You have a specialty, and you stick to it. I'm what the humans like to call a 'jack of all trades'. I love to learn about everything and anything, even if it's only just a little."

"Okay, well. I really should get going. Thanks for everything."

He smiles. "No problem. I'm sure I'll be seeing you at some point before long."

Chapter Sixteen

ADRESTIA

After Vaelyn left me in the alley, I decided to go straight back to my apartment. I couldn't bring myself to work on the case, even if that means another woman shows up dead. It'll be my fault, but I don't care at the moment.

Dejection is a bitch, and I'm taking it really fucking hard right now.

As much as I want Vaelyn to stay, I won't keep her against her will. She's a free spirit, and I know I couldn't confine her because I've felt the same way before. My family held me back for far too long when all I wanted was to be free.

When I get to my door, dread settles like a weight in my chest. My apartment is going to be far too quiet, and that's the last thing I want, especially after last night. Memories already play on repeat in my mind of the time we spent together.

I fling the door open and don't even make sure it gets closed before I'm stomping across my penthouse—I just want to collapse in my bed. The moment I end up on it, I instantly regret my decision. My sheets still smell like her. I know I should make myself get up, but instead, I bury myself in her scent.

What can I say? I'm a glutton for punishment.

The sound of my balcony door sliding open wakes me. I hadn't even realized I'd fallen asleep. Flying out of my bed, I head for the living room. Who would dare come in here without my permission?

I walk down the hall, preparing for a fight, but I stop dead in my tracks. Standing before me is the woman who hasn't left my mind. She's in her harpy form with what looks like silver lightning streaks spread across her exposed skin. Her platinum blonde hair perfectly matches the feathers of her wings, which are currently wrapped around something in her arms. I take a step closer and realize that it's actually a woman curled up against her chest, covered in a blanket.

My heart leaps into my throat. "What are you doing here?"

"Let's wait for Avyanna," she says.

At the mention of my mimic, my heart skips a few beats. "Who's that in your arms?"

"Put two and two together, Adrestia. I know you can."

I purse my lips. "Why did you bring the gorgon here?"

The woman in question shifts in Vaelyn's arms. "Believe it or not, this is the safest place for me right now. I want to be here just as much as you want me here."

"I have no problem—" I begin, but another figure walks in through the front door that apparently didn't get closed when I came in earlier.

The hair on the back of my neck stands, and I prepare for the worst. When the person steps into the light, I come face-to-face with... myself? What the fuck?

Vaelyn huffs out a laugh. "It's just Avyanna."

My front door slams shut, and the woman parading as me steps forward. Every single piece of her looks just like me, all except one single thing—an all too familiar beauty mark on her cheek. As I look her over, the woman slowly starts to change, her features becoming ones I know like the back of my hand.

I shake my head. "Why did you choose me?"

Avyanna shrugs. "No one would question your walking into your own building. I've never been here, so that would be a little suspicious, especially not being chaperoned by someone who does live here."

"That's fair," I say. "Can someone please tell me what you're all doing here?"

A shimmer flashes over Vaelyn, bringing her back to her human form. She eyes me as she folds herself up on the couch with the gorgon still in her lap. It's an interesting sight, seeing as Vaelyn is several inches shorter than the gorgon.

The gorgon adjusts herself in Vaelyn's arms, and Avyanna takes a seat beside them, placing a hand on the gorgon over the blanket. There's a heavy tension hanging around them. What the hell happened between the time we all left that alley and now?

I take a seat in the chair across from them, placing my elbows on my knees. My eyes drift over each of them, starting with Avyanna. Her eyes shift from me to the door every so often while she rubs small circles with her fingers over the blanket covering the gorgon. She's trying to portray a calm exterior, but those ice-blue eyes swirl with a mix of emotions I know how to read all too well. Being here is making her uncomfortable.

Beside her, Vaelyn is glaring daggers at me. Her stormy grey eyes haven't left me since she walked in. And she's gripping onto the gorgon like her life depends on it. Why?

Speaking of the woman in Vaelyn's lap, she's curled up so tightly that I'm not sure she'll be climbing out anytime soon. Avie looked pretty protective of the gorgon when we were in the alley, so I wonder why she's attached to my harpy now.

We sit in silence for a few more moments before I've had enough. "Someone tell me what the fuck happened."

Avyanna's jaw clenches. "We needed somewhere safe to bring Roxi after she was abducted off the street and raped by three of her father's guards. This is where Vaelyn suggested we come. We suspect the guards have been following us since she left, so I didn't want to go back to my apartment."

"Why the hell does her father have guards?" I ask.

Avyanna scoffs, while Roxi shifts in Vaelyn's arms so she can face me. "He hired them after I was born—because of what I am. Who knows if he was protecting me from the world or if he was protecting the world from me, though. When he died a few decades ago, the guards just stayed. They've pretty much left me alone until last night. That's when Avyanna got me out of there."

"That's strange," I say. "I'm sorry for what's happened to you. We should look into these men and figure out what their prerogative is with you, why they're trying to find you when your father isn't even technically employing them any longer."

"Honestly, I'm really fucking tired right now and would love to get some sleep," Roxi says with a yawn.

"I have a guest bedroom in the back with a bathroom attached. You're welcome to use those while you're here," I say.

Vaelyn stands with Roxi still in her arms. "I'll get her settled back there. I'm quite tired myself."

Avyanna moves to follow, but Vaelyn shakes her head, so Avyanna sits back down. My mimic crosses her arms over her chest and sits back. I mirror her movements, pursing my lips because I'm not even sure what to say to her.

"Our dear friend Alaric sends his regards," she finally says.

"I'm not sure if I should be glad he's nearby or worried," I say flatly.

"He did tell me something interesting."

I lean forward, curiosity getting the best of me. "And what's that, Avyanna?"

Her eyes lock onto me. "That you're the reason I got away from those sex traffickers when your family sold me off."

My heart leaps into my throat. "Is that so?"

"Yep." Then, there's a long pause before she asks, "Is it true?"

"Do you think that little of me?" I ask, ending with a laugh of disbelief. "Of course it's true. I couldn't stand by while they hurt you. *Used* you. What my family did to you was beyond fucked up, and I'll never forgive them for it. I cut ties with them after that. The biggest reason I didn't come after you when you escaped was because I wanted to give you space, plus it gave me time to track down the remainder of the sex traffickers and kill them so they'd never hurt another again."

Emotion flickers through her beautiful eyes. "Well, fuck," she whispers.

"I could never expect you to forgive me—it never should've come to that. The expectation was for me to choose them. To their displeasure, I chose you, so they tried to take that choice away from me. They had you abducted while I was away so that I couldn't interfere."

Tears fill her eyes. "You did choose me?"

"Absolutely. I would've chosen you one hundred times over, even if it ended the same way. My family never truly cared about me, and that whole situation made it clear," I say, dropping my gaze to the floor.

We sit there in silence for a long while before she asks, "Addie, do you believe in soulmates?"

Her question catches me off guard. I lift my gaze to meet her eyes and raise an eyebrow. "Something of the sort. Griffins speak often of Animae Gemellae—twin souls. They say you know when you find them because you never want to be away from them. You feel complete."

She purses her lips as her brows draw down. "Did you ever believe they existed?"

"I've known very few griffins who say they've found their Animae Gemella. I want to believe they're real—because of the way I feel about you and now Vaelyn after such a short time—but I've never been good enough for anyone, especially my own family."

"That's not true," she says, sniffling. "Before your family fucked up our relationship, I was so madly in love with you it made me sick. You made me feel like I finally had somewhere I belonged, someone with whom I belonged. My kind believe in something similar to the griffins: Sielunkumppani. It's Finnish, meaning soul companions."

I stare at her for a moment. "Why are you bringing this stuff up now?"

"When I told Alaric that Roxi could look all three of us in the eye, he asked me if I knew the term soulmates. Of course, I told him how I feel about it—the term

is over-hyped and overused in the human world—but
he said soulmates are a huge deal in the supernatural
world. Every species just has its own name for it. He
told me gorgons call them Synkairós or Synkai for
short."

"Let me guess, the gorgon could look their Synkairós
in the eye."

She nods. "Exactly. And there have been cases of a
gorgon having multiple Synkai."

"So you think we're all her Synkai? That we're all
connected somehow?"

She nods again. "I think it's a possibility. Especially
since we all have such strong feelings toward each
other in such a short amount of time."

I sigh. "This feels like something out of one of
those books the humans read. They go feral over 'fated
mates'."

Avyanna laughs—the sound is so beautiful and
melodic. I wish she'd do it more often, but I know she's
been through so much in her life, and it's hard for her
to see the good around her sometimes. I love the way
her blue eyes light up and her cheeks flush when she's
happy. If she'd let me, I'd make her happy for the rest
of our lives.

She catches me staring at her and peers out the
window that overlooks the city. "I really wish things
hadn't happened the way they did. Honestly, I would've

rather had you come after me and explain things, not let me run away and think you'd possibly been part of your family's plan."

"I wanted to give you space. You'd just been through a lot because of my family. When I felt like I'd given you enough time, though, you were already gone. I didn't want to chase you, so I left it alone until we ran into each other," I explain.

"Well, we can't change the past, but we can shape the future. Let's get some rest and pick this conversation back up in the morning, okay?"

A smile creeps across my face. "I'd love that. It sounds like we've got a lot to discuss as a whole. Should we go see how Roxi and Vaelyn are doing?"

Chapter Seventeen

Vaelyn carries me down the hallway, and I'm perfectly content here. She already makes me feel safe. But I'm sure I look really awkward curled up against her as she carries me. I'm at least a few inches taller than her, not to mention I'm sure I'm a bit heavier than she is.

When we make it to the bedroom, she asks, "Sleep first or a bath?"

Knowing I likely still have blood caked on me, I say, "I think I'd like a bath."

Without another word, she walks straight past the bed into a bathroom that rivals the one at any of my father's mansions. The vanity's counter is made of pure black marble with flecks of gold, and the toilet beside it is the darkest black porcelain I've ever seen. Across from them is a shower tiled in black and forest green, which seems almost coincidental considering the green of my eyes, along with the scales of my snakes. Beside that is a massive black marble tub I can't wait to climb into.

"I can draw my bath," I say.

"No, let me, please. I want to take care of you. You've been through far too much this evening. Drawing you a bath is the least I can do."

Tears line my lids as she sits me down on the counter. "Thank you," I whisper.

She cups my cheeks, pulling my face down, and gets on her tiptoes to kiss my forehead. "Of course. I'll get it started for you."

Her hands are gone all too quickly, and I immediately miss her touch. Tonight has been absolutely awful, and I just want to curl up in someone's arms where I know I'll be safe. Even though things are a little strange right now between us all, I'd honestly take the ability to climb into bed with any of the three women in this penthouse.

Every single part of my body hurts; I'm hoping this bath helps with something. From what I know about gorgons, we're supposed to have increased healing times, but I've never had to find out whether it's true. I guess today is as good a day as any.

When she starts the water, I chance a look at myself in the mirror behind me. I still clutch the blanket around me, covering my shoulders and most of my neck, but above that, a faint bruise circling my neck catches my eye from where the bag rested. My eyes drift further up to my cheek, where there are distinct finger marks from when one of the men covered my mouth. Moving further up, I meet my own eyes in the mirror and gasp. The whites of my eyes are nearly all red with numerous blood vessels having blown, which intensifies the green of my eyes. And then there's my hair; it's going every which way thanks to the bag having tangled it up and the flight here with Vaelyn not having helped any.

I stay like this until I spot Vaelyn approaching me through the mirror. Turning to face her, I drop my eyes to the ground. I'm ashamed of how awful I look.

"Your bath is ready. Can I help you down?" she asks.

"Sure. Thank you," I whisper.

She moves to lift me off the counter, and I try to tell her she doesn't have to, but she shoots me one of those looks that means I'm not supposed to argue. I concede and wrap my arms around her shoulders while she carries me to the bathtub. It seemed so far away when I was on the counter; however, it only takes her a few strides to get us there.

"I'll set you down and turn my back so you can unravel yourself from the blanket and get in. I just want to make sure you get in there safely before I head back into the bedroom," Vaelyn says.

"You can stay. I kind of don't want to be alone right now," I say.

Vaelyn puts me on my feet and turns my cheek to look at her. "You're safe. No one would dare come into Adrestia's penthouse. If you're not comfortable with my being here, I'm happy to wait until you're done. All you have to do is—"

I bring a finger to her lips. "It's okay. You can stay. You likely saw me naked when you helped save me. Even if you hadn't, I'm not shy."

The blanket falls from my shoulder, but her eyes are on mine. Warmth spreads throughout me, and I let go of the blanket in full. I want her to touch me, erase everything that happened to me earlier in a place I thought I was safe. My free hand snakes around her neck to cup the back of her head, and I bring my lips to hers, giving them a soft kiss before whispering, "Tell me to stop."

"I'm the wrong person to ask that of. Because I'm going to tell you *not* to stop," she says, her lips brushing against mine with each word.

I don't hold back anymore, crashing my lips to hers. Every ounce of rigidity rushes out of her. Her arms slide around my back, pulling me until there's no space between us at all. I melt into her touch and deepen the kiss, a frenzied need taking over me. My hands roam down her back, finding the hem of her shirt, and I slip underneath.

About halfway up, she stops me. "You need a bath and some rest."

Resting my forehead against hers, I whisper, "I want you to touch me, to erase everything those men did to me."

"Are you sure? You don't want Avyanna? She's already explored your body to an extent, so she'll know what you like and what you need."

"I'm sure. I want you. But if you don't want to do this, you don't have to."

She steps back, her brows furrowed as she looks me over. "More than anything, I don't want to hurt you. You have so many bruises, and I'm sure a lot of them hurt. The last thing I want to do is add to them or make things worse."

I reach for her hand to pull her to me, but she resists. "You won't hurt me any more than I already am. Unless you want to."

She frowns, looking me over once more. Her eyes darken, and I know she's letting the lust win her over.

"I wish I could kill the fuckers that hurt you all over again."

"They'll be gone before too long. Get in the bath with me. Please?"

Her stormy grey gaze locks onto me. "Fucking hell. I can't tell you no already, and that's going to be a huge problem."

A smile spreads across my face.

She huffs out a breath and steps in closer to me. "Get in the bath like a good girl while I get undressed."

My pussy clenches. "Where's the fun in that? I want to help you."

I bat my eyelashes at her as I slip a hand under her shirt again. Our skin contact makes her jump—my hand is quite cold—but she quickly recovers and leans into me.

"You're quite the brat, aren't you?" I nod, and she continues, "Since you're already there, why don't you take my shirt off for me?"

My smile widens when I bring my other hand under her shirt, making her jump again. Once she relaxes, I slide my hands up her sides. As I reach her ribs, I prepare to run into a bra, but she's not wearing one, so just to tease her, I cup her breasts and pinch her nipples.

Her mouth falls open in a gasp. "Roxi," she growls. "You're injured, and I'm *trying* to take care of you."

I roll my eyes and release her nipples. "You're not being any fun."

"You're being a brat, and that normally deserves a punishment, but like I've said, I don't want to hurt you."

My hands leave her body and fist into her shirt, yanking it up over her head. "Don't worry about whether or not you're going to hurt me; just do it."

"You've been hurt enough today."

"Then make it so the pain I feel has a more recent, pleasurable memory. Don't hold back just because you don't want to hurt me," I say, fumbling with her pants.

Her hand rests on mine, and I stop to look up at her. "If you're serious about this, I want you to give me a safe word. Don't hesitate to use it if things become too much."

I stare at her, contemplating what word I could use. "Bomb Pop."

"Bomb Pop? Like the popsicles?"

"Exactly," I exclaim. "They were my favorite growing up. My father said they were healthier for me than regular ice cream because, for whatever reason, he cared about my physique. Now, for yours."

She rolls her eyes again. "I don't—"

I narrow my eyes at her. "You do need one."

A sigh leaves her lips. "Bananas."

My eyes widen, and I start to laugh, but Vaelyn's jaw is clenched tight.

"Yes, it's bananas, and you don't have to sing the song," she huffs.

"So cranky."

Once again, she rolls her eyes. "I'm a harpy. We're nearly all grumpy. And you're getting in that bath to soak and clean up before anything else. Now, get in there before I pick you up and put you in there myself."

Chapter Eighteen

Avyanna

Adrestia and I walk down the hallway in comfortable silence until Roxi squeals, which sends my heart rate skyrocketing. The griffin and I exchange a look before we're barreling through the bedroom door to make sure everything is okay. When laughter drifts in from the bathroom, I will my heart to slow even though I know it won't until I lay eyes on Roxi and Vaelyn, so I make my way into the bathroom.

What I find has me stopping dead in my tracks just after I cross the threshold. Roxi, having discarded the blanket, is completely naked, straddling a still fully clothed Vaelyn in the bathtub. And fuck if it isn't hot.

Adrestia approaches from behind and stops right behind me. Her hands come to rest on my hips as she whispers, "I'd say you find this just as appealing as I do with the sudden burst of your arousal that just filled my nostrils."

I groan, and Roxi's gaze drifts up to where we stand. Vaelyn's gaze follows shortly after, those stormy eyes flaring wide when she realizes Adrestia and I are standing here. "I-I, uh. She—"

"We don't have to explain ourselves to them," Roxi whispers, biting Vaelyn's earlobe while she stares me straight in the eyes. "I think they'd like to watch us pleasure each other."

I clench my jaw, my arousal heightening. "Roxi, you're injured."

Roxi bites her lip. "I don't care right now. I need someone to replace the harm those three monsters did to me."

Adrestia kisses my neck, her arousal hitting me hard. When we were together, we never shared partners, but the four of us being together just feels different... right. I think it has to do with what we've discovered, that we're all tied together, and there's nothing wrong with us wanting each other.

"This tub isn't big enough for the four of us. Get cleaned up and come to my room. Avie and I will meet you guys in there," Adrestia growls as she turns me toward her and throws me over her shoulder. "It's been far too long since I've worshipped this body, and I'm not going to waste any time in getting started. Fuck, this is going to be beautiful."

"Addie! Put me down unless you want to be bitten," I hiss.

She laughs and starts down the hall to her bedroom. "That doesn't scare me off, Avie. If anything, it turns me on more. You know I love it when you bite me."

I let out a low growl, which just has Addie laughing again. "It's too bad I can't really bite you in this position, because I would."

Addie scoffs as she rounds the corner into her room. "Well, if you really wanted out of this position, you'd get yourself out. Don't act like I'm not aware of your skills."

When I open my mouth to respond, Addie pulls me back over her shoulder and throws me down on her bed. All the air rushes out of my lungs upon impact, making me see stars, but that doesn't stop Addie from ripping my clothes off.

"Be careful of my gear!" I wheeze.

"I'll buy you more. I need to feel you, make sure this isn't just a dream," Addie says.

Rolling my eyes, I push her back, but she doesn't budge. "This isn't a dream. My gear comes off easily. Let me sit up and help you."

She takes a step back, eyes narrowed at me. "I'm impatient, Avyanna."

"You're not going to be impatient when I knock your ass out. Chill," I growl.

"Fuck, you're so fucking feisty, more so than you used to be," she says.

I flash her a devious smile as I stand. My fingers make quick work of all the clasps and buttons—I've been wearing this same gear for years, so I've learned the ins and outs of it. With each piece of gear that hits the floor, Adrestia's eyes darken further and further.

When the last piece slides off my body, Adrestia is on me, her lips crashing against mine, and her fingers skimming across my skin. My hands slide up her shoulders into her hair, grabbing a handful of the golden strands. She growls, trying to resist my hold, but I yank harder.

"You're still dressed, and I don't think that's very fair," I say.

"I don't care what you think is fair right now. I want to worship your body like I've always been meant to. Now, lie down on this fucking bed and let me taste you before I break out the ropes to make you," she growls, nipping at my lip.

My pussy throbs, begging for the attention, so I let her guide me back onto the bed and release her hair.

Once I'm lying back on the bed, her mouth returns to mine, giving me gentle kisses.

Breaking our kiss, she whispers, "Good girl," and then kisses down my jaw to my collarbone, where part of my serpent tattoo is. "This is new. When did you get it?"

"A few decades ago, after I lost sight of Roxi. It starts at the nape of my neck, where the tail weaves into my hairline, because my obsession with her started with a single look." As I explain, she kisses along the tattoo, across my chest to where my heart is. "The scales are the same as those of her snakes, just as the eyes are the same color as hers."

"Why are its fangs bared right above your heart?" Adrestia asks, her lips brushing against my skin with each word.

"Because she sank her teeth into me and took a piece of my heart when she disappeared on me."

Adrestia's eyes meet mine. "Damn, now I'm hurt because you didn't do anything like that for me."

I roll my eyes and bring both of my wrists up so she can see the tattoos there. "I got these a few years after I escaped and left you behind. This one," I say, gesturing to my left wrist with a small, black cartoonish heart impaled by a dagger, "was the first one I got. It was to remind me what love had done to me the first time I tried to pursue it." Then, I point to my right wrist, which says 'Temptation is a monster' in a gothic script. "I got this one a short time after because I almost went off the deep end. I missed you so fucking much, and I thought about trying to find you, but I kept telling myself this, to remind me in a way that following temptation can lead to your demise if you're not careful."

"That's not as cute as the one for Roxi," she says, brows furrowed.

I drop my wrists to the bed and shrug. "They both have similar meanings. You both weaseled your way into my heart, and each of you left me in different ways. But now we're all together with another to complete us."

She kisses my sternum to hide her smile. "Since when did you become an optimist?"

"Since I've discovered the people who make me feel whole."

Chapter Nineteen

Vaelyn

When Adrestia carries Avyanna out of the room, my attention turns back to the beautiful woman straddling me. "Things are about to get really fun. Let's get you cleaned up so we can join them."

Roxi sighs and moves to push off my lap, but I wrap my arms around her. "I need to get this blood off. I'm not even sure whether it's mine or someone else's at this point."

I pin her with a stare. "I said 'let's' not 'you need to', which means I want to help you."

She mumbles a quick 'okay', and a feeling of triumph washes over me. Reaching over to the shelf beside us, where several generic bath products sit, I grab a loofah without taking my eyes off Roxi. Then, I dunk it in the water and glide it over Roxi's exposed skin to get it wet. She arches into my touch, causing her hips to shift against my pants. A gasp leaves her beautiful lips that I want nothing more than to capture with my own.

Running my tongue piercings over my lip, I switch the loofah to my other hand so I can grab the body wash. Squeezing a healthy amount onto the loofah, I bring it back to Roxi's skin. My eyes follow the path of the soapsuds, admiring the creaminess of her pale skin. When I get to her chest, I spot a wound I hadn't seen before and stop. I study it for a moment, noticing how smooth the edges are, how superficial it is.

Fury surges because not only did those fuckers rape her, they marked her skin for their enjoyment.

The warmth of Roxi's hands cupping my face brings me back to her. "Hey. What's wrong? Your feathers are starting to come to the surface at the nape of your neck."

Leaning forward, I kiss the cut on her chest. "I wish I could've stopped them sooner, before they hurt you so bad."

She sighs and rests her forehead against mine. "We can't do anything about it now, but you can help me forget for a little while."

"I'll do anything, Rox."

When we finally get Roxi cleaned off, she climbs out of the bath and finds us some towels while I disrobe. My clothes are completely soaked, so it makes it that much harder to get them off. Roxi ends up helping me because she's just as impatient as I am. She has every right to be, though. If the other two are anything like me, we're going to do everything in our power to overwrite all the pain.

As soon as the last of my clothes is off my body, I scoop Roxi up and carry her into Adrestia's bedroom, where they've already gotten started. Avyanna lies on the bed, splayed wide open with Adrestia devouring her, while she plays with her pierced nipples. I groan. Two out of three of these women have pierced nipples. I'm looking forward to playing with them.

Avyanna's back bows off the bed with a loud moan. She's getting close.

I put Roxi on the floor quietly and whisper in her ear, "Go sit on Avyanna's face."

Roxi bites her lip as she looks up at me, excitement dancing in her stunning eyes. Then she creeps across the room to the opposite side of the bed, climbing up and capturing Avyanna's lips with hers. Avyanna's hands release her nipples only to reach for Roxi's. A gasp leaves Roxi, breaking their kiss.

Avyanna moans again, but whispers, "Come, sit on my face," in a seductive tone.

Roxi complies, and Adrestia licks Avyanna's clit one more time before she turns to me. "Are you just going to stand there, or are you going to join the party?"

"I'm trying to find the best place for me to go," I say.

"You have a couple of options, but I think Roxi deserves the most attention right now," she says, gesturing toward the gorgon.

I raise an eyebrow. "Do you not get to be pleased? Because the way I'm looking at it, you're pleasing Avyanna, but no one is pleasing you."

Adrestia licks her lips. "This is plenty pleasing enough for now, little one."

"Fine," I say with a grin cresting my lips. "Where are your toys?"

The griffin's eyes darken. "In the closet. Go past my shoes to the mirror and press the button. It'll open up my collection. Grab anything you want. I'll be grabbing some more later."

Without another word, I stroll into the closet, following her directions. When I find the mirror, I press the red button, which opens up to another room. Nearly every kind of toy you could imagine lines the walls, all arranged by type, color, and function—in that order. Adrestia definitely seems like the one to have a Type A personality, and this proves it.

I wander around the room, moans filtering in from the bedroom, looking for the toys I want, all while grabbing some that just look intriguing, and some that are going to drive these women crazy. By the time I'm done, I've grabbed so much that I struggle to carry everything to the room without dropping something.

Adrestia's eyes widen when I exit her closet, and I giggle. "You have a lot of stuff in there. Hell, you may as well have your own freaking red room with everything you have."

She releases suction on Avyanna's clit. "You haven't seen everything this bedroom has to offer. The loops for the ropes are only the beginning."

My cheeks redden, and I lick across my lips with my tongue piercings. "I'm very intrigued."

"I think you'll be experiencing it sooner rather than later with that attitude you always have," she says.

Maintaining eye contact with her, I take everything over to the bed and drop it all beside Avyanna, who's so lost in Roxi's pussy that Roxi is screaming. Then, I pick up the specific toy I grabbed for Adrestia: a remote-controlled vibrator.

Her eyes darken when she sees what I'm holding. "And who is that for?"

"You. Because while I'm on the opposite side of the bed fucking Roxi's pussy with your favorite toy, I'm going to be controlling your orgasm with this," I say, holding up the remote to the toy in my hand.

"I like where this is going," Adrestia purrs.

"Good," I say, placing the toys back on the bed. Then I grab a couple of other small vibrators as well as a clitoral clamp. I place them beside Avyanna's ass so Adrestia can easily reach them. "Just in case you want help making her come."

"Aren't you so thoughtful?" Adrestia says, looking over the toys I brought her.

"I can be," I say as I kneel beside her.

Then I capture her lips, tasting Avyanna's sweet arousal, while I unbutton her pants and slip my hand in to prep her for the toy, although I'm sure she's soaked already. My fingers slip between her folds, slickness immediately coating them. Adrestia gasps when my fingers swirl around her clit, jostling her piercing, but I slip my fingers further back to find her entrance. The second I find it, her walls clamp around my fingers, desperate for the fullness.

Biting her lip, I pump into her. "Such a good girl. This was exactly what you needed. Now I want you to show Avyanna just how good I'm making you feel."

With a nod, she returns to Avyanna's pussy, and I watch, enthralled by her movements. Avyanna's muffled moans increase against Roxi's center with the return of Adrestia's mouth, making me crave an ounce of the pleasure they're feeling.

I allow myself a few more pumps into Adrestia before I slip my fingers out and maneuver her pants down so I can put the toy inside her. When I slip it inside, she groans. Then I click the button to turn it on, and she jumps, but it quickly turns to a moan.

Satisfied, I grab the rest of the toys and make my way to the other side of the bed. Roxi is thoroughly enjoying herself, low moans leaving her lips as Avyanna works her pussy. She's leaned forward on her hands, trying not to suffocate Avyanna, while her hair cascades around her face toward the bed.

I bring my hand to her lip, pulling it from between her teeth. "How does it feel to be sitting on Avyanna's face, Rox?"

"So fucking good. I've already come, but she won't let me up," she pants.

"We want more than one orgasm from you tonight. Sit up and give her one more. You're not going to hurt her; she'll tell you if you do," I say, tilting her chin up to look at me. "Can you do that for me?"

Roxi nods and sits up, resting her hands on her legs, so I praise her. Avyanna grips her hips, pulling Roxi down onto her mouth more than before, making Roxi's mouth fall open on a moan that I capture with my lips. She has no clue how much better this is about to get.

While I kiss Roxi, I put all the toys down except a pair of nipple clamps with a chain between them. Since they're slide clamps, I loosen them all the way before taking one of Roxi's breasts in my hands. I massage it for a moment before finding her nipple and pinching it. She moans again, breaking our kiss as she throws her head back.

"I think you're going to enjoy this, but if I hurt you, please tell me," I say just before clamping her nipple and tightening it.

Her mouth falls open in a silent scream as her entire body tenses, and she falls apart. After a moment, a mix of screams and pants leaves her until she collapses forward against me, unable to hold herself up any longer.

"That was unexpected," I say.

Her eyes flash up at me, the intensity of the green ebbing. "You don't say. Holy fuck."

With a wicked smile, I pick up the double-ended vibrator and say, "I'm going to fuck you with this next."

Chapter Twenty

My eyes widen as I look at the toy Vaelyn is holding. "I don't think I'm going to be able to take any more."

Vaelyn laughs. "You will. But if it gets to a point you can't, you have your safe word." Then she kisses my ear and my neck. "You wanted us to replace everything they did to you; let us do that."

Avyanna kisses the inside of my thigh and wiggles out from underneath me. "That reminds me, we all need safe words and all need to know what they are so we can stop if things become too much."

Vaelyn rolls her eyes. "I have never—"

My gaze turns severe as I push away from her. "You heard her. We *all* need safe words. That includes you." Looking at where Avyanna and Adrestia sit, I say, "My safe word is Bomb Pop. Yes, I know it's technically two words, but I don't care."

Adrestia holds back a laugh. "You young-uns."

Avyanna shoots her a look. "I'm the oldest one here. Knock your shit off."

"Maybe your safe phrase should be 'get off my lawn' or something like that," Adrestia mumbles.

Avyanna rolls off the bed and grips Adrestia's cheeks. "Would you like to say that again to my face?"

"Not particularly," Adrestia says to the best of her ability. "But you should hear what Vaelyn's is. It's actually rather adorable."

Releasing Adrestia's face, Avyanna gives her a quick kiss before turning to look at Vaelyn. "Color me curious. What's yours?"

Vaelyn rolls her eyes again. "Bananas."

Avyanna shakes her head. "Addie has always loved music, so I'm guessing she made the joke about the Gwen Stefani song."

I laugh because I was about to make the very same joke when she told me. "Okay. That's two out of the four of us. Adrestia, Vee, what are yours?"

"Sounds like my time to shine," Adrestia says proudly. "My safe word is cattywampus."

Vaelyn, Avyanna, and I all burst into laughter while Adrestia pouts.

"It's my favorite word," Adrestia says when the rest of us begin to calm down.

"That's actually one of the best safe words I've ever heard," Vaelyn says, tears rolling down her face from how hard she was laughing.

"All right, Vee. You're last. What's yours?" I ask.

Lips tipped up, Avyanna says, "Red."

Adrestia grunts. "Seriously? You're so basic!"

Avyanna shrugs. "Sometimes simplicity is bliss."

"Now that we've settled that," Vaelyn says, swooping in to kiss and suck on my neck.

I weave my hands into her hair as she descends lower toward my unclamped nipple. When she reaches it, she takes it into her mouth, swirling her tongue around the stiffening peak. I throw my head back and moan, catching sight of the other two who're working on getting Adrestia undressed.

After one more lick of my nipple, cold metal clamps onto it. I sharply inhale, arching into Vaelyn's touch.

"That's it, Rox. Do you like that?" Vaelyn asks, kissing my breast. I nod, not sure if I can form words at the moment, but she tuts at me. "Use your words."

"Yes," I pant. "It hurts, but in the best way possible."

"Good girl," Avyanna whispers, coming up behind me, her hands resting on my hips.

I lean into her, giving Vaelyn access to more of my body. She takes advantage of it, kissing and nipping as she descends lower.

When she makes it to my pelvic bone, her ass is up in the air, and I have the urge to reach out and smack it. But then she looks up at me through her lashes, those stormy eyes laced with lightning.

"Fuck, you look gorgeous with those clamps on. I think we need to get them pierced," she says, voice husky.

Adrestia climbs onto the bed behind Vaelyn and smacks her ass. "Do you have a thing for nipple piercings, little one? I saw the way you reacted when you realized mine were, and I smelled your heightened arousal when you saw Avyanna on the bed with me between her legs."

Vaelyn looks back at Adrestia. "And what if I do? I think they're hot as fuck."

"Maybe we need to get yours done, then," Adrestia says, smacking Vaelyn's ass again.

"Sign me the fuck up," Vaelyn says. "Piercings and tattoos are fucking sexy."

Adrestia's lips tip up into a sly grin as her hand slides down the curve of Vaelyn's ass. I bit my lip, watching the scene before me when Avyanna grazes the fingers on one of her hands down my hip, between my thighs.

She parts my folds, finding my clit with ease. Vaelyn and I moan at the same time.

Avyanna nips at my neck again while her other hand wraps around my throat. "I want to taste your blood so bad, but you need your strength."

I tilt my neck so she has better access to it. "Do it. I want you to."

"You're fucking perfect," she growls against my skin, sending shivers through my whole body.

Then she strikes, sinking her teeth into my neck. At first, it feels like a hot iron searing me, but then pleasure rushes through me. My mouth falls open on a moan, which quickly turns into a scream when she continues strumming my clit. Something between a hum and a growl rumbles in her chest as she retracts her fangs from my skin, the first drop of my blood hitting her tongue.

Her hand tightens on my throat, and she leans me back against her more. I let her, willing to do anything she wants as long as this continues, but I'm caught off guard when I feel something furry between my thighs. My eyes fly open, trying to figure out what it is.

"Adrestia is beating me to fucking you. Brat," Vaelyn says with a laugh in between moans.

My brows furrow, but then I hear a click, and Adrestia curses just before there's a loud smack on Vaelyn's ass. Vaelyn hisses on impact and laughs shortly after.

"I almost forgot you had that in until I saw the remote," Vaelyn says to Adrestia.

"Fuck," Adrestia whimpers, holding tightly onto Vaelyn's hips.

"If you let me turn around, I'll lick your clit to get you there faster," Vaelyn says, waggling her eyebrows.

Adrestia smacks Vaelyn's ass again as the furry thing moves out from between my thighs and flicks in front of me, moving toward Adrestia's face. That's when I realize what it is—her tail, which is now coated in my arousal. Sticking her tongue out, she swipes her tail over it to taste me. As weird as it is, it's actually pretty arousing to watch.

"Mmm. You all taste so delicious. I call eating you out next," Adrestia says, looking me directly in the eyes.

I whimper, and Avyanna's pulls slow on my neck. Her suction releases, tongue sweeping over the wound her teeth created to seal it. "Adrestia, lie on the bed like I was before so I can eat your pussy. Roxi, sit on her face, but face me so Vaelyn can fuck you with that toy at the same time."

Vaelyn pushes up from the bed, eyes alight. "Hell yes. This is going to be fucking amazing."

Chapter Twenty-One

ADRESTIA

Vaelyn shoots up, tossing the remote for the toy in my pussy toward Avyanna. My mimic's hand slips out from between Roxi's thighs to catch it with a sly look on her face. I'm fucked—literally—because she's going to torture me with it. I shoot Vaelyn a look and whimper when Avyanna changes the setting on the toy. Vaelyn and Avyanna laugh simultaneously, so I flip them both the bird.

"One of these days, I will fuck you with this toy the way you did to me on our first night together," Vaelyn says, reaching to help Roxi off the bed.

My tail swishes behind me while I eye Vaelyn and wait for Avyanna to get off the bed. "You and that damn mouth. I'm going to put it to work soon."

When everyone is out of my way, I get myself situated, the toy in my pussy still vibrating. With each change of position, it hits a different spot, and I have to stop what I'm doing for a moment. Avyanna doesn't let up on me either. If anything, I swear she changes the setting at least once while she watches me squirm. Once I finally make it to my back, someone yanks me to the edge of the bed. Looking down, I'm met with ice-blue eyes, pale skin, and wavy black hair—Avyanna.

"You're all such brats," I mumble, moving my tail out from underneath me.

"You just don't like it when someone else bosses you around," Avyanna says.

"None of what has just occurred was someone else bossing me around. That was just plain mean," I say, staring down at her.

"Aww, does the griffin need to use her safe word?" Vaelyn asks.

I roll my eyes. "Roxi, get your ass up here."

Hesitantly, she crawls toward me, but before she can get too far, I grab her by the throat and bring her in for a kiss. She moans into my mouth, parting her lips just slightly, so I slip my tongue in to deepen the kiss. Avyanna changes the setting on the toy again, and I gasp, grabbing Roxi's throat tighter, which she seems to enjoy. When I loosen my grip, she bites down on my lip, hard enough that she draws blood.

She laps it up, sucking on my lip for a moment before pulling away. "Your blood is decadent."

"I doubt it's as decadent as your pussy. Climb that sexy ass up here so I can test my theory," I say.

A radiant smile lights up her face. "If we're testing theories," she says, reaching her hand between my thighs, "I'd like to see if this tastes as good as—or better than—your blood."

Her fingers begin to rub over my clit, but then she stops, her eyes widening. "Is your clit... pierced?"

Vaelyn comes up behind Roxi and kisses her shoulder. "It is. And so is mine. Except mine is in a little bit of a different position."

Roxi rubs my clit, playing with the piercing. "I have a lot of questions, but I must say I like it."

Vaelyn laughs. "Later, Rox. Right now, you need to test your theory and then sit on Adrestia's face."

"Spoilsport," Roxi mumbles, removing her fingers from my clit and sticking them directly into her mouth.

Her eyes roll back as she sucks every last drop of me off her fingers. "I don't know if I can pick a favorite of the two."

"You can compare later," I say, pulling her in for one last kiss.

Vaelyn smacks her ass when Roxi doesn't move fast enough, causing the gorgon to yelp, but it gets her ass in gear. She positions herself above me, trying to hover like she'd done with Avyanna. That doesn't fly with me. Wrapping my arms over her hips, I pull her down onto my mouth and suck her clit into my mouth. She falls forward, hands landing directly on my breasts, while I go to town.

Behind her, Vaelyn already has one end of the toy inside herself. I watch as she preps the other end, putting lube on it—even though I'm fairly certain she won't need it because Roxi is already so wet—and then sidles up behind Roxi.

Placing her hands on Roxi's hips, Vaelyn says, "Are you ready?"

"Get it inside me already," Roxi pants.

"You don't have to tell me twice," Vaelyn says eagerly.

From where I lie, I get a front-row view of Vaelyn notching the toy at Roxi's entrance. She's ready for it, her cunt trying to clamp down on what little of the toy is inside her. Ever so slowly, Vaelyn pushes in. Roxi's grip on my breasts tightens as the toy inches in.

"Fuck, this feels too good," Roxi whimpers.

The toy inside me changes again, and I grab Roxi tighter.

"Sounds like we'd better get Adrestia there, too," Avyanna says.

Releasing suction on Roxi's clit, I pant, "I need you to play with my clit, Avie."

Avyanna obeys, spreading my legs and kissing down my thighs as she kneels on the floor. When she reaches my pussy, I wiggle my ass. Avyanna tsks, smacking my clit. Then she increases the intensity of the vibrator again.

"Patience, Addie," Avyanna hisses.

I roll my eyes and go back to playing with Roxi's clit. Vaelyn is pumping into her slowly now, trying to get the toy fully in. It's distraction enough that I forget how desperate I am for Avyanna to play with me until her mouth is on me. My back bows, enjoying myself.

We stay like this for a moment, all the while my tail is seeking out Avyanna. It winds around her leg, creeping between her thighs. She hums a moan onto my clit, making me even wetter. When my tail finds its destination, it plays with Avyanna's clit. She's always loved having her clit played with; it gets her to the crest that much faster. I've always wondered why she's never gotten her clit pierced.

When Vaelyn has the toy fully seated in Roxi, she turns the vibrations on. Roxi lets out a scream while Vaelyn groans. Their increased pleasure has me working on Roxi's clit faster. I want her to get there before anyone else.

"Come all over this toy, Rox—squirt on Adrestia's face. Show us how good this feels," Vaelyn says, pumping into Roxi hard and fast.

"I'm going to come," Roxi screams, spurring both Vaelyn and me on.

With one more thrust, Roxi comes undone, her arousal coating the toy and seeping onto my face. Vaelyn follows shortly after, then me, and lastly Avyanna. We all stay in place, shaking while we come down from the incredible heights we each reached.

Something feels different between us all, in the best way possible.

Vaelyn is the first to move, pulling the toy from Roxi and turning it off so she can take it out of herself. Avyanna follows suit, turning the toy off inside me before she removes it.

Roxi collapses on the bed, still panting, but I lift her into my arms and begin walking toward my ensuite bathroom. "Shower. All of us. We're all sweaty, and I want everyone clean before they climb into my bed."

Thankfully, Vaelyn and Avyanna follow without complaint.

The next morning, we wake up all tangled in each other, still naked after our shower last night. Vaelyn is curled up against me on one side, while Avie lies on my other, with Roxi nearly lying on top of her. Crazy enough, the only thought that's going through my mind is that this is perfect. If it were up to me, we'd never leave this bed.

I'm about to drift off back to sleep when my phone starts ringing. I try to ignore it, letting it go to voicemail, but it rings again. I mutter a few quiet curses as I unravel myself from the others to get to my phone, hoping it's not who I think it is. Relief washes through me when no one stirs, but I still hurry into the kitchen to grab my phone.

I groan quietly when I see who it is: Bella—just who I thought it would be. When I hit the button to answer, she doesn't even give me a chance to speak. "There've been two more bodies found with the same MO. S.I.R

.E.N. is about ready to call in the D.A.M.N.E.D. if you don't figure this shit out quickly."

"It is too early for you to be yelling at me like this," I whine.

"Adrestia!" she yells. "It's already fucking noon."

That perks me up. "Why didn't you call me sooner?"

"Because I only just got the call myself."

"Alright. I'll get it figured out ASAP. Luck is on our side because one of the D.A.M.N.E.D. is staying with me, so I'm hoping she can help find whoever is doing this faster. I'll keep you updated, B. Promise."

"Umm, I feel like there's something I'm missing here. There's a hunter staying with you?" Bella asks, voice rising.

I have to hold my phone further out to keep from blowing one of my eardrums. "B, it's not the time to have this conversation. I need to get ready and wake her up so we can get over there."

Bella groans. "Fiiiiine. If you need more backup, let me know, and I'll get some out to you. But you *have* to tell me," she says, knowing how I am.

"I'll be fine, B. Let me get myself going and I'll get to the crime scene—"

"Crime scenes, boo. There are two, and I'm warning you now that the unsub seems to be escalating. The scenes are totally different, but it seems like the same

MO. I fear that whatever is doing this will only get worse the longer they go unchecked."

I take a deep breath and pinch the bridge of my nose. "Fuck. Okay. I'm going to focus as much attention as I can on this."

She sighs. "Look, I don't know what you're up to, but I need you to make this your number one priority until we find the unsub. I really need you to do everything you can to prove B.I.T.E. has what it takes to protect humans and supernaturals alike. If there's even one more death, S.I.R.E.N. is taking the case from us, which could be our downfall."

"I know, B. I'll get it taken care of."

"Thank you, Addie. Love you."

"Love you too. I'll text or call in a bit," I say, then hang up.

Two more bodies in such a short time is definitely concerning. The fact that things have escalated is even more so. I need to get my ass going, so I toss my phone onto the kitchen counter and head back into the bedroom.

The first thing I notice when I enter is that Avie is missing from the bed. Both Roxi and Vaelyn are still fast asleep, cuddled up to each other. It's kind of cute, to be honest. I stand there and admire them like some sort of creep until I hear the toilet flush, so I wander into the bathroom, where I find Avie at the vanity washing her hands. She's still as naked as the day she was born, and I fucking love it. Her curves make my mouth water every single time I see them.

"Who called you so early?" she asks, voice still raspy from sleep.

"My boss, Bella. And apparently it's already almost noon. She said there've been two more bodies found, and I need to go check everything out. S.I.R.E.N. is threatening to give the case to the D.A.M.N.E.D. if another body is found, so I have to figure this out before that happens. Bella did say she's worried the unsub is escalating because these two scenes are so different."

Avie dries her hands and turns to face me. I have to force myself not to look at her impressive tits... or the rest of her body. "What can I do?"

"Help me find whatever is doing this. Two sets of eyes are better than one. Plus, you're insanely smart, hence why you're a hunter."

She rolls her eyes. "I study patterns and track my targets. Being what I am, my sense of smell is nowhere near as enhanced as yours, but I'm able to pick up on different things. I guess what I'm trying to say is that I use my strengths to my advantage and keep my disadvantages in mind, so I'm aware of what my limits are. That's what it takes for me to be a hunter, not my 'smarts.'"

I stare at her for a moment in awe. She quirks an eyebrow, and I just huff out a laugh. "You're incredible. I wish you could see that for yourself."

She waves me off. "Whatever you say. Let's wake up the others and let them know what's going on."

After getting dressed and barely keeping our hands to ourselves, we wake Vaelyn and Roxi. Both of them are fairly hard to rouse, which makes me laugh. Of course, my harpy wakes up grumpy, but that's nothing new for her.

Once everyone is upright, I explain the case's rapid progression over the last few days. Roxi looks like she's going to vomit as I explain the women's injuries in detail, but I continue anyway. When I'm done, everyone sits there, staring at me.

"Why are Roxi and I staying here? More eyes means a higher probability of finding this… *thing*," Vaelyn says, irritation seeping into her voice.

Avie answers, "Because Roxi isn't used to this sort of thing. We need someone to stay here with her, and I feel it should be you because Addie and I both do this for a living."

I sigh. "I agree with Avie. The more eyes, the better, but when there's someone inexperienced—sorry, Roxi—it can cause hiccups in the investigation."

Vaelyn huffs. "You're right, but that doesn't mean I have to like it."

Roxi pulls her knees to her chest and wraps her arms around them. I move toward her, but she shakes her head and scoots herself against the headboard. Tears well in her eyes as she says, "Vaelyn is right. The more of you looking this over, the better, and this thing needs to be taken care of. No one has to stay here with me."

Across the bed, Vaelyn's brows furrow. Climbing onto the bed, she places a hand on Roxi's knee. "I want to stay here with you. They can let us know if they need our help. Why don't we whip up some breakfast while we wait for them to come back? I'd say we can order in, but I don't really have money."

I take my credit card out of my wallet and hand it to Vaelyn. "Get whatever you guys want. Don't worry about how much it costs, either."

Vaelyn's brows furrow further. "I-I can't."

"Why not?" I ask.

Her nostrils flare wide. It seems I've struck a chord. "Because I don't need you to take care of me."

Leaning forward, I grip her chin with my free hand. "I'm not doing this because I have to; I'm doing it because I *want* to. I *want* to take care of you, even though you don't need it. I *want* you here with us because having you in my vicinity makes it feel like a piece of me has returned when I didn't know it was gone in the first place. Being with you three has made me feel the best I have in a long time."

Vaelyn rolls her eyes, and Roxi snags the credit card from my hand, saying, "You guys go take care of the case. We'll be here waiting for you. Although I'm going to order more than just food. Avyanna, Vaelyn, and I don't have clothes that fit here because, let's face it, you're a hell of a lot taller than we are."

I lean forward to kiss Vaelyn before I release her chin. Then I beckon Roxi toward me. She climbs across the bed eagerly, stopping right in front of me. My fingers sweep a piece of hair that's fallen in her line of sight, and I kiss her lightly. "Please do. Whatever your heart desires. But just know I'd rather watch you all walk around here naked."

Avie and I make our way to the most recent scene in silence. We haven't discussed what she said about the four of us being soulmates of a sort since before everything happened last night, but I feel a hell of a lot more connected to the others since our escapades. My clit comes to life at the thought, and I cuss myself out internally because we're almost to the scene.

As we approach, I notice that this courtyard is nearly identical to the one where Avie ran into me. It feels like it's been forever since that day already.

S.I.R.E.N. is just finishing up securing the area, while a couple of supes stand guard just outside the entryway, dressed like ordinary police officers to draw less suspicion. Unlike Avie, I'm not able to tell what kind of supes they are, so I approach with caution.

"They're just shifters. You're fine. Nothing to worry about from them," Avie whispers.

I relax a little and continue toward them. "Good morning. I'm here with B.I.T.E. to assess the scene."

One of the men scoffs. "Didn't realize your organization was in such desperate need of help that they recruited a hunter. You're really weaseling your way in there, aren't you?"

Avyanna steps forward, anger rolling off her in waves. "I am here of my own volition. The D.A.M.N. E.D. do not own me, nor have they ever owned me. I'm a free agent and can do as I please. If you don't believe me, contact them for yourselves, but I don't see how this concerns you either way."

The shifter takes step after step backward to avoid Avyanna, but he runs into a wall as the last words leave her lips. Color drains from his face, and it takes everything in me not to laugh at the man. There's a reason you don't piss off my little mimic: she's dangerous, and everyone knows it.

I walk up behind her and grab her by the waist. "Now, now, Avie. You can't eat the shifter just because he mouthed off to you." She instantly relaxes into me, and I flash the shifter a sly grin. "But since we've cleared the air, we'll head into the scene. Have a good day, boys."

Chapter Twenty-Two

Vaelyn

oxi and I lie in bed for a bit longer before our bladders scream at us to get up. We each take our turns in the bathroom before crawling back into bed. It's so comfortable that all I want to do is fall back asleep, but Roxi's stomach rumbles, so I get up and look around for a laptop—we all know Adrestia has to have at least one.

I've never actually looked around the penthouse. The first time I was here was when Adrestia literally ran into me. You know the rest of what happened that night. Then, when we got here last night, I was so focused on taking care of Roxi that I didn't pay much attention to my surroundings. This morning, I'm trying to be a lot more cognizant of everything.

I enter the hall from Adrestia's room, looking both ways so I can decide where to start first. Down the hall to my right, everything is dark, and all I see at the end of the hall is the door to the guest bedroom. To my left, the sun shines brightly through Adrestia's million and one windows, illuminating a small portion of the living room. I head down that way, passing a few other doors that lead to a half-bath, a linen closet, and a laundry room that has no business being anywhere near as big as it is.

The last doorway I come to doesn't actually have a door on it, so I step in, and my eyes widen. The first thing I notice is bookcases lining an entire wall, filled to the brim with books of all kinds. I'm instantly drawn to it, admiring the spines of books ranging in age from those that are almost falling apart to those that are glossy and unmarred.

This is something I never would've seen in the nest. The elders dictated every single aspect of our education, down to the books we read and the supplies we used.

When I come to the old wooden desk, I smile. It's one that has the rolltop lid over it and several drawers with metal handles. My fingers skim over the well-polished wood before they find purchase on the metal handle at the opening. I barely bump into it, and it opens, causing me to jump back a little. I certainly didn't expect it to be automatic, given its antique look.

As it lifts, my eyes land on the exact thing I was looking for: a laptop. I don't even wait for the lid to open all the way before I'm unplugging the laptop and snatching it to scurry back to Roxi. I've been away for long enough that I'm sure she's starving by now.

Walking down the hall, I say, "Sorry, Rox. I got distracted. You should see all the books Adrestia has in her study. Or is it called an office? I have no clue. But I did find her laptop!"

Her laughter filters down the hall toward me. "I think you need to get laid more often. You're so much happier when you do."

I laugh as I walk through the doorway. "Honestly, I think most people are happier when they get laid."

She rolls her eyes, and I throw the laptop on the bed just before I tackle her. Her shriek pierces my ears as I land on her, both of us still very naked, but I love the feel of her skin against mine. I bury my face in her neck, peppering it with kisses, and she squeals.

"Vae, stop! I'm hungryyyyy," she whines.

"I have something you can eat."

She shoves me. "That satisfies another type of hunger, not this one."

I sigh. "Fine."

"Thank you. After we order food, we're buying clothes. And I'm not buying cheap shit, either. Addie did say money wasn't an issue, after all."

Roxi orders food from three different places. *Three different places.* She said she couldn't choose what sounded best, so she just ordered it all. As we all know, I've never lived like this—having loads of money to spend on whatever I want. I'm trying very hard to look at everything through a different lens, but it's difficult for me.

While we wait, we move on to shopping for clothes. She knows all the places to order from and asks for my input, especially when it comes to clothes for me, which I appreciate. In the end, just buying clothes for the two of us, we spent well over five thousand dollars.

"Did we really need to spend that much?" I ask.

"Of course we did! We deserve the best out there. Plus, we needed all of our clothes to get here sooner rather than later, right?"

I shake my head and shrug. "I mean, I guess?"

She smacks my arm. "No, no. Not 'I guess'. You need to know because you deserve everything you could ever want. Sometimes you need to work for it, but that doesn't mean you don't deserve it any less. I'm going to teach you some confidence."

I roll my eyes. "Good luck with that."

Her eyes level on me when the doorbell rings. The sound takes a second to register, and once it does, her eyes light up. I melt into a puddle on the bed, deciding I want to see that look on her face constantly. How I'm going to achieve that is beyond me.

She tosses the laptop onto the bed, and hurries to climb off. On her way out, she grabs a shirt from the top of Adrestia's laundry, yanking it on. I let out a small laugh again and fall against the bed.

What did I do to get here? Whose good graces did I get into? I've found three women who want me, three women who make me feel like I belong with them. It seems too good to be true.

That peace is ruined when the front door opens and a man says, 'Oh, fuck'. Then Roxi screams, and I'm flying out of bed, already shifting into my harpy form before my feet have the chance to hit the ground. I reach the living room just in time to see a man stepping past another that's turned to stone. He throws a bag over Roxi's head and starts to drag her toward the elevator. The idiot doesn't make it far before I'm grabbing him by the throat with one hand while I rip into his chest cavity with the other, tearing his heart out in one swift movement. He lets go of Roxi—who falls to the floor—and then disintegrates to ash in my hands.

"What the fuck," I mutter before shifting back and turning my attention to Roxi.

She's managed to rip the bag off her head and pushed herself against a wall. Tears stream down her face as she rocks back and forth. I clamber up to her, cupping her face in my hands.

"Did you know him?" I ask quietly.

She nods. "H-he was o-one of my g-guards."

"Fucking bastard. Do you know what he was?"

"A v-vampire. It's why he turned to ash when you ripped out his heart."

"Did you know the other man?"

She shakes her head. "It looked like he had a bag in his hand, so I think he was delivering something."

"Shit. We need to get you inside before anyone else shows up. May I carry you?" I ask, needing her permission. She's been manhandled *again* by some asshole who thought he could do what he wanted with her.

All she does is nod before I lift her in my arms and rush past the man who's been turned to stone. When I get to the bedroom, I lay her on the bed and kiss her forehead before pulling on the first shirt I see so I can deal with the man in the hall.

I start off by grabbing the bag from his hand—well, actually, I have to literally rip it from his grasp—so I can take it inside. Taking care of the man himself turns out to be harder than I anticipated, though. He's nearly a foot taller than me, and now he weighs several hundred pounds since he's stone. Even in my harpy form, he's hard for me to manage.

I finally have the man halfway through the door when the elevator dings. Muttering out a quick, 'Son of a bitch,' I shove past the man and hurry into the penthouse so I can return to my human form.

A woman's voice yells out, "Hello? I have a delivery here."

I rush back down the hall, still only wearing Adrestia's shirt, but fully in my human form. "I'm so sorry. One of my friends sent me a statue of himself as a gag gift, and I can't seem to get it through the damn doorway. You can leave the stuff right by the door, and I'll grab it shortly. Thanks!"

A bag rustles as it's placed by the door. "Umm, okay," a woman says, skepticism filling her tone, before scurrying back down the hall.

When the elevator dings again, I slip past the statued man to make sure no one else has come up. Roxi ordered from three different places, and only two have delivered thus far. Since the elevator is around the corner, I wait for a moment.

It's a good thing I do because a young man who's probably about as tall as I am hurries around the corner carrying a massive box, nearly tripping over his own two feet. He spots me, and I can sense his heartbeat quickening. Then I spot the growing bulge in his pants. I internally groan, but flash him a fake smile.

"I, uh, I'm sorry I'm late," he says, his voice much deeper than I expected.

I give a small laugh and hold out my hands to take the box from him. "Not to worry. Someone else just delivered something, so I was already standing out here. My girlfriend is starving, so she ordered from a few different places."

His pupils dilate, I'm sure, thinking about the fact I have a girlfriend—although I'm not even sure if that's what you'd call us. It's most men's wet dream to watch two girls give each other pleasure. If only he knew there's actually four of us; he'd have a heyday with that.

As he puts the box in my hands, his brush against mine, a rush of energy passes through me. I take a step back, running directly into the statued man. All feeling leaves my body, and I crumple to the floor.

The last thing I hear before I lose consciousness is the man whispering, "I'm sorry it had to happen this way."

Chapter Twenty-Three

Avyanna

As we walk into the courtyard, my stomach roils. It's one of the most gruesome crime scenes I've ever come to—and I've been to far more than I can count at this point—but this is one I'll likely never forget. It's definitely a striking difference from the scene I came across when I first arrived in the city.

My eyes drift around the courtyard, taking in every detail. While the woman I saw at that first scene only had claw marks across her body, the poor woman here has been ripped limb from limb. Parts of her body are littered around the space, and her blood is on nearly every surface imaginable. They're going to be cleaning this up for hours, if not days, to keep the humans from asking questions.

I leave Addie where she stands to take a closer look at the body parts. The torso lies in the center, claw marks covering nearly every inch. Because there are so many, most of her organs are splayed out around it. From what I remember at the scene I was at, this monster has been eating his victims, but this one has no organs missing. Moving on, I look over all the other body parts to see if anything is missing. Interestingly enough, every single piece of this woman is accounted for.

Grinding my teeth, I return to Adrestia. "Did you say there's another scene?"

Adrestia sighs. "Yep. That's what I've been told. This one was closest to the penthouse, so that's why we came here first."

"I need to see the other one before I can say anything for sure."

"Let's head there then," Adrestia says.

When we get to the other scene, I prepare myself for the worst again, but I'm relieved to find that it's nothing like the one we just left. Similar to the first scene I saw, this woman was ripped open, but this time the perp got their fill. What remains of her entrails hangs out of her open abdomen and spills onto the ground below her.

We can't determine which woman died first because the other was dismembered, which cools down the body much faster. But if the perp killed this one first, why the hell would it attack a second woman in such a short amount of time? It'd gotten its fill from this one.

After looking around, I grab Adrestia's hand and drag her away from the scene. "Addie, I'm not sure this is the same perp."

Adrestia shakes her head. "Avie, think about it. All the women look similar, the claw marks are identically spaced apart on each victim, and they've all been found in courtyards."

"Ignore that for a moment. Think of the difference between this scene and the other. This is our supe's normal MO. The other scene is one of desperation, a loss of control…" I pause to look back at the woman who's finally being taken away. "I guess what I'm trying to say is that if it is the same supe who attacked both women, not only are the attacks growing closer together, but they're escalating. We don't have long to figure this out if it's the same perp."

"Yeah, I know," Adrestia says with a sigh. "Let's go back to the penthouse so we can try to piece some things together."

For the first time in years, I'm glad to be away from a crime scene. Hunting monsters has been my life for so long; now I just want to enjoy some time with my girls. It feels weird to call them that, but after last night, everything feels different. I feel whole in a way I never have before.

But the moment we walk into Adrestia's building, something feels off. I look over at Adrestia, and her furrowed brow tells me she feels it too. We rush to the elevator, smashing the button as if that'll summon one faster.

When one finally shows up, we impatiently wait for the people aboard to vacate. I breathe a sigh of relief when no one else tries to come on the elevator with us. They must sense the unease rolling off us in waves.

The entire ride up is excruciating. It feels like an eternity before we finally arrive on Adrestia's floor. Terror clutches my heart, squeezing impossibly tight at what we'll find when we get to the apartment.

Adrestia doesn't even wait for the doors to open all the way before she's squeezing through and running down the hall. I'm right on her heels, trying to keep up with her long strides. But when she rounds the corner, she stops dead in her tracks. I collide with her, nearly toppling us both to the ground.

I right myself quickly and peer around her. The air rushes out of my lungs as panic seizes me.

Vaelyn lies on the ground, still as a statue, and I can't even tell if she's breathing.

Adrestia lunges forward, collapsing onto the floor beside her. A sob rips through her as she pulls the harpy into her arms, cradling her limp form. Vaelyn's chest rises and falls, telling me all I need to know at the moment.

My eyes shoot to the apartment door, panic seizing me again. Not only is the door wide open, but there's something massive halfway through the entryway. I creep toward it, unsure if the person who attacked

Vaelyn is still around, and halt when I realize what it is.

A man.

Who's been turned to stone.

Throwing all caution to the wind, I dart into the penthouse, looking through each and every room for Roxi. But she's not here.

Chapter Twenty-Four

I startle awake, sitting straight up, only to find myself in an all too familiar place: my bedroom at my father's house. Panic creeps up my throat in the form of a scream, but I tamp it down.

This has to be a nightmare; I can't be here again.

My eyes scan my surroundings. With the lights off, I can't see as much, but I've occupied this house for at least a year, and I've memorized every aspect of this room in that time. There isn't an item out of place from the last time I'd been in here.

Then I remember that Avyanna attacked Merric the night she'd rescued me. I scramble to the edge of the bed to look for any sign of blood, but there's nothing. The putrid scent of his blood was here when I'd been brought back yesterday, hence why they took me to the guest bedroom. Plopping myself back onto the bed, the silk sheets glide against my bare skin. I'm naked, just as I'd been after my shower the night I 'left' here.

Were the last few days a whirlwind of a dream that I conjured up? I've always wanted to leave the protection my father supplied, to see what was outside and interact with others.

I allowed myself to get lost in everything that has happened since the night Avyanna 'saved me'. I'm so lost in my thoughts that I almost miss the shadows in the corner of my room shifting. I spring to my feet in an instant, not caring that I'm nude. The man who walks out has my jaw hitting the floor and questioning everything from the last few days harder than ever. I thought Avyanna had killed him.

Merric's eyes roam over my body, being careful to avoid my eyes. "Here we are again. This time, there's no one to save you, though. You'll be mine like I've always wanted you to be."

My body quivers, full of equal parts rage and fear, which causes me to transform into my gorgon form. Sounds like I hadn't dreamed up the last few days after all.

Courage trickles through me with that realization. "Is that so? Tell me that again as you look me in the fucking eyes!"

In the blink of an eye, he's throwing me to the floor, flat on my back, with him pinning me down. He shifts my hands so they're pinned above me and shoves my legs apart with his knees, his thick length grazing my clit. I buck my hips, trying to throw him off, but it's useless. He's massive. And stronger than I thought he'd be.

Something between a growl and a snarl erupts from his throat, making my heart rate shoot through the roof. "Stop fighting it, Roxanna. You're mine now, and no one will be able to take you from me."

"No! Get off me!" I scream.

The same kind of growl bubbles in his chest, slowly leaving him as he thrashes his head back and forth above me. There's something wrong with him, but there's nothing I can do while I'm pinned beneath him, so I decide to take another approach.

With several deep breaths, I coax my body to return to my human form and speak to the demon atop me with the most soothing tone I can muster. "I'm sorry.

You really scared me, and you're hurting me. Can you please let me go?"

His grip loosens, but he doesn't move. "You're going to try to leave again."

"No, I won't. I promise. Please, Merric," I beg.

He hesitates for a moment before releasing my hands and sitting up. This position has his cock nestling against my entrance. All he'll have to do is rock his hips forward, and he'll enter me, which is the absolute last thing I want right now.

His gaze lazily sweeps over my exposed body, and all I want is to cover myself. Something about him has me on edge, but I can't place what it is. I'm also still scared as fuck to move.

"Can I please get back on the bed? I'm getting rather cold," I say quietly.

"I would rather fuck you on this floor to keep you warm," he says, lip curling.

My heartbeat skyrockets again. "Wh-why? The bed is far more comfortable for your knees as well."

He shakes his head. "I need to claim you before he takes over, like with all the others. He says you're the only thing that can fix me, keep me from becoming the monster he wants me to become."

Terror sends a shiver down my body. What in the fuck is he talking about?

I don't get a chance to ask him. His body begins to tremble, and his eyes widen in terror. A series of 'no's' spills from his lips as he shuffles back, clutching his head between both hands. His eyes fall shut, and when they open again, they're different from any I've ever seen. The whites have turned completely black, while the irises and pupils have become the color of rubies.

Shooting to my feet, my gorgon form takes over again. Whatever is happening to him isn't good in the least, and I need to get out. Those intense eyes meet mine, but nothing happens to him.

Something is very wrong. I'm frozen in place, and he knows it.

His head tilts to the side with a weird, all-too-creepy smile on his lips. Then I watch in horror as his glamour falls, revealing an emaciated-looking version of the man I'm familiar with. A scream builds in my throat, desperate to be released.

Merric laughs wildly and climbs to his feet on limbs that are far longer than they should be. "You're more perfect than anyone deserves. The only reason I told him you would fix him was because I want you for myself. I'm sure you're going to be the most delectable thing I've ever tasted, and I can't wait to sink my teeth into your flesh."

My body moves of its own accord, sending me hauling ass down the hall toward the stairs. I've never been so scared in my life. Whatever Merric has become isn't natural, and I don't doubt that if he gets his hands on me, he's going to do exactly as he said. I won't let that happen.

Shoving down my fear, I force myself to recall my human glamour. When it's fully in place, I curse the fact that I'm not wearing any clothes because I can't run through town completely naked. If I do, I'll draw a lot of attention, and that'll risk people looking me in the eye.

Thankfully, when Vaelyn flew me to Adrestia's penthouse, I chanced a few looks at the ground, so I know there's a patch of trees on the way there. I hope I can run into one of the three women whom I want nothing more than to be with right now. They have to have noticed I'm gone by now.

Once I'm down the stairs, I glance around, looking for a blanket at the very least. Noticing one on the couch, I snatch it and wrap it around myself. Merric lets out another snarl as he clambers down the stairs, kicking my ass into gear. I have no clue how fast the fucker is in this form, nor do I want to find out.

I'm out the door in seconds flat with Merric mere feet behind me. I hightail it toward where I think the trees are. As soon as my bare feet hit the blacktop, the stones in the pavement dig into the soles of my feet.

I try with all my might to ignore the pain because if Merric captures me, I'm dead.

His harsh breaths are the only things that fill my ears as I run. I'm sure it's because his proximity is my primary focus, but either way, it motivates me. I run faster than I ever have, even when Avyanna chased me.

When I finally reach the trees, I weave between the trunks, trying to throw him off. His abnormally long limbs have him running into tree after tree, and relief washes over me. It's slowing him down—just what I wanted it to do.

My relief is short-lived, though, when he lets out that nasty snarl again. Trees begin crashing down after that, narrowly missing me. This was a bad idea.

Taking a chance, I make a sharp turn, heading toward the city again. Maybe if we get into the city, he'll be forced to fall back. If the humans see him, it'll cause far more problems for the supernatural community than anyone wants to deal with, but it might save me at least.

Ahead of me, the trees thin, and a car zips down the street. I rush forward with renewed invigoration, hope spurring me on.

I'm almost there when abnormally long arms wrap around me, a hand clasping directly over my mouth as I try to scream. My hands release the blanket covering me and go straight for the arms, digging my nails into the flesh to get away.

A winged creature lands before me, and my heart leaps. Within seconds, another creature lands beside the first while a figure on the ground appears on the other side. All three figures before me step forward, and the light hits their faces.

It's them. The ones I can always count on.

Avyanna—the one who saved me from a life I didn't know I needed saving from, even though she didn't truly know me.

Vaelyn—the one who has accepted me, even when she was scared to do so.

Adrestia—the one who has given me a safe haven when I was in danger, even though that danger came to her front door.

After mere days, I know these women are everything I could ever need and more.

Chapter Twenty-Five

ADRESTIA

I step toward Roxi and this monster I've never seen, but Avyanna grabs my arm. "Addie, don't get too close."

"What is it?" I ask as Roxi screams and writhes against the monster, nearly ripping out my heart.

A tremor runs through Avyanna. "It's a Wendigo. They're extremely uncommon, but very dangerous. He seems to have lost—"

The monster snarls again, taking a step back. "Leave, or I slit her throat while you all watch."

Avyanna's hand on my arm changes suddenly, the skin rippling. "That would be the last thing you ever do, Merric. I will kill you where you stand."

"You're going to kill me anyway because of what I've done. I may as well go out with a bang, am I right?" the monster says with a sinister smile, his mouth inching toward Roxi's neck.

As he gets closer, Roxi's eyes widen, and she stills. Then, some sort of knife flies out from Avyanna's direction, striking the Wendigo directly in the eye. He releases Roxi and claws at the knife. Vaelyn rushes forward, scoops up Roxi, and then takes off, getting our beautiful gorgon out of here.

The Wendigo roars, drawing my attention back to him. He's managed to dislodge the knife along with his eye, leaving only the oozing, sizzling socket behind. That's got to hurt like hell.

"You bitch!" the Wendigo screams at Avyanna. "You'll pay for that."

Avyanna laughs. "And how will that be? You'll be dead as soon as you confirm what I think you've done."

I look back and forth between the two, but stay rooted where I am. Avyanna is the expert monster hunter; I'm just here for back-up at this point.

But the Wendigo fucks up my plans when he lunges for me. Avyanna and I both spring into action, but she gets to him first. In a flash of movement, she's plunged the same kind of knife—if not the same one that was in his eye—into the Wendigo's spinal column. He falls to the ground, paralyzed from the waist down, unless that knife is removed.

He snarls again, hands flailing to reach for his back. Avyanna stomps down on one of his arms, and I follow her lead, doing the same with the other. His claws catch my attention, so I stare at them for a moment.

"Thank you," she says to me. Then, she puts more pressure on his arm and leans forward. "You killed those women in the courtyards over the last few days, didn't you?"

My brows furrow, still staring at his claws. From what I can tell, they're at least of a similar distance to the ones on the women. Could this really be our unsub?

With a menacing laugh, he confirms her suspicions. "What can I say? He needed to feed me to keep me at bay. Then, when he gave me a taste of her, she became the one I wanted. But you took her from me that night and then again when my men brought her back to me."

I step down harder on his arm, and he screams. A bone cracks, causing his hand to fall limp. "You're disgusting, and you deserve to die."

"He couldn't handle it anymore. She was just too good to pass up. Once we tasted her pussy, it was all over, and I had to have her. Fuck, that one taste was delectable, though. I'm sure her flesh would've been far better," he says, sealing his fate because if Avyanna doesn't kill him soon, I will.

As if she can read my mind, she says, "Not yet, Addie. He deserves to be tortured for what he's done."

A growl rumbles in my chest. "He does, but we need to check on Roxi, too."

"She's safe with Vaelyn," Avyanna assures me.

"Fine," I huff. "Where are we taking him?"

"Back to where this all started," she says, a Cheshire grin spreading across her face.

Once we finally have the Wendigo back at the mansion, we drag him down to the basement and string him up from the ceiling. The knife is still in his spinal cord, so he hasn't been able to fight, but trust me when I say that I've been worried about it falling out since we started back because it's been sizzling like his eye socket had.

We're finishing up the last knots on his ankles when metal clanks against the cement. The knife finally fell out. I'm barely able to step back before he's thrashing in his restraints. Avyanna rolls her eyes and steps forward, pressing a finger to each restraint with a few mumbled words. As her hands leave each one, they start to glow.

She's blessing them.

When she finishes with the last one, she comes to stand beside me and crosses her arms. "Every basic demon has the possibility of becoming a Wendigo when it consumes flesh. It's not something they need to survive—it's a luxury. The more they lean into that craving, the harder it gets to resist. Once it starts, there's no stopping it, though. When they get this far, they tend to latch onto specific targets and will do everything in their power to have them."

My lip curls as I stare at the Wendigo. He stops thrashing and flashes me an unsettling grin. I shake my head. "You realize this is the end for you, right?"

He snarls and snaps at me, showing off his jagged teeth. "It's not over until it's over."

Avyanna snaps her fingers at him. "Over here, Merric. You will die by my hand today, but I have questions first."

"I'm not answering shit," he hisses.

A smile crests Avyanna's lips as her hand rounds her back. In the blink of an eye, she's retrieved a knife and flings it at the Wendigo. It lands in the meatiest part of his shoulder, which has him howling in pain. The sizzling starts shortly after. Whatever metal the knife is made from is literally dissolving his skin and everything underneath it. Bile rises in my throat, but I take a deep breath to settle myself.

"You'd better get used to this blessed iron then," Avyanna says, her face devoid of emotion.

"Fucking bitch. That fucking hurts," the Wendigo hisses.

Avyanna laughs. "That's the fucking point."

"Fine. What do you want to know?" he asks.

"Where are your men?" Avyanna asks.

The Wendigo's eyes glint as he stares her down. "Not here, clearly."

Another knife whizzes from Avyanna's hand into the Wendigo's other shoulder. "No shit, Sherlock."

The Wendigo hisses in pain, his flesh beginning to dissolve from the new knife. "They're on another assignment."

"See," Avyanna coos, "that wasn't so hard now, was it?"

"Fuck you," he hisses.

Avyanna tuts. "Now, now. If you continue to act like that, you're going to get further acquainted with my knives." He huffs out a breath, but stays silent, so she continues, "What kind of assignment?"

"Protecting another high-profile client," he says.

"Why have you guys continued to protect Roxi after her father died?" she asks.

"Per her father's request. He paid us for the next hundred or so years," he explains.

Avyanna grinds her teeth hard enough that I can hear it from where I stand. "Will they continue to come after Roxi?"

The Wendigo laughs. "They could give a shit less at this point. After you killed my men last night, they want nothing to do with the bitch. We have better, less dangerous, and more willing clients to attend to."

Avyanna's jaw ticks hard. "Are your men also Wendigos?"

"I don't fucking know!" he yells.

Lifting an eyebrow, Avyanna reaches behind her. "Attitude."

The Wendigo rolls his eyes. "Some of them are demons, but I'm not sure if they've partaken of flesh or not. It's not exactly something I ask on their fucking application."

Avyanna's hand whips around her, and another knife embeds itself into the Wendigo's chest, just above his heart. He howls out in pain, thrashing in the chains again. "For fuck's sake! Just fucking kill me already."

"You don't deserve a quick death," she hisses, skin rippling as she steps toward him. "You didn't give any of the women you murdered quick deaths, did you?" His heated gaze bores into her while he shakes his head. "Exactly. You will suffer just as they fucking did."

"Get it over with then!" the Wendigo screams.

Reaching behind her, Avyanna withdraws two smaller blades made of the same material as all the others from her belt. I swear, all these blades make me think she's some sort of Mary Poppins because they're coming out of nowhere.

She gets in his face with those blades at her sides, and the Wendigo snaps at her. I start to jump forward, but her hand swings up, plunging one of the blades under his chin. His eyes flare as blood pours from his mouth.

Then she rips it out and hisses, "That's for trying to take what is *mine*. Everything else I do will be for the women you hurt."

The Wendigo tries to snarl again, but all the blood in his mouth makes it sound like a weird gargle. Satisfaction surges through me because I know he's nearing his end. After my mimic does her thing, he'll never hurt another again.

I watch as she takes her time with him, running the blades across his arms, just deep enough that it has blood bubbling to the surface, but not enough that blood flows freely from the cuts. When she gets to his shoulders, she jams the blades already there deeper. The Wendigo hisses in pain, but he's near the point of losing consciousness. Avyanna must know because she plunges one of the small blades into his side. Adrenaline rushes through his body again, and he jerks upright. She laughs and leaves the blade there. Her now-free hand wraps around the knife in his chest while her lips tip into an evil smile. She yanks it out, and then her smile widens. In one swift movement, she sinks the knife into his belly and rips it up to his sternum. His organs spill out onto the floor, and his mouth opens as if he wants to speak, but blood pours out.

"We all know this isn't enough to kill you, but you won't heal because you haven't been fed," Avyanna hisses in his face.

A wet breath leaves his mouth, but my mimic isn't done yet. She takes the other small blade and slowly pushes it into the Wendigo's chest, right where his heart is. His skin sizzles as he looks down at it.

"This blade will be the only mercy you find from me. As it dissolves your skin and flesh, it'll get closer and closer to your heart. Once it reaches your heart, that's when you will die. Until then, you will suffer," Avyanna whispers.

My jaw drops all the way to the floor. She's even more ruthless than I thought she would be.

When she turns to face me, I school my features, but I see that prideful gleam in her eyes. "Let's go check on our girls."

Chapter Twenty-Six

Vaelyn

I make the flight back to Adrestia's penthouse as quickly as possible because Roxi is shivering non-stop in my hold. I'm not sure if it's because she's cold or because she's in shock over what happened to her. Again. Either way, I want her to know that she's safe, forever and always, with Avyanna, Adrestia, and me.

When I land on the balcony, I wrap my wings around Roxi in a cocoon of sorts, trying to warm her up, and head straight for Adrestia's ensuite bathroom. "I'm going to draw you a hot bath so we can get you warmed up."

She shakes her head and clings to me. "I don't want a bath. Just... hold me, please?"

I stop and glance down at her. Tears fill her eyes as she stares up at me. My heart aches for her, knowing she's been through a lot lately, so I kiss her forehead and whisper, "Whatever you need, sweetheart."

"Thank you," she says, voice cracking halfway through.

Continuing into the bedroom, I say, "Anything for you. Always."

The climb onto the bed is challenging, not only because I'm holding her but also because this bed was made for Adrestia and her height. Still, I manage to make it on without having to put Roxi down. I settle myself in the center and lean up against the headboard. Roxi readjusts herself until she's found a comfortable spot and falls asleep in my arms.

I stare down at her while she sleeps for far longer than I realize, but I'm brought back to reality when the bedroom door flies open. My arms tighten around Roxi, and I prepare to fly us to safety. Somehow. Rich amber eyes lock with mine, and every thought of running leaves my body. I relax back into the bed, a breath of relief leaving me.

Adrestia climbs onto the bed before me, taking my face in her hands. She kisses me roughly and desperately, like she never thought she'd get to do it again. Avyanna rushes up beside her and shoves her out of the way so she can claim my mouth in an intense, possessive kiss, which leaves me breathless. When her mouth leaves mine, she brushes a gentle, yet affectionate kiss on Roxi's brow while Adrestia rolls her eyes.

My eyes fill with tears as I let out a breathy laugh. "There's no need to fight over us. While I may be the smallest of us, I will kick both of your asses. Roxi needs rest. And food at some point. She never got to eat her breakfast."

Avyanna looks to Adrestia before glancing back at Roxi and me. "You're right. But I won't ever stop trying to show all three of you how much you mean to me. In such a short time, you three have shown me what life is all about. You've all made me realize what I've been missing in my life. When I'm with you, I finally feel like I belong—like I'm not the outsider everyone else makes me out to be. Adrestia gave me a taste of that long ago, but I think we were meant to separate so we could all find each other. I've always believed everything happens for a reason; you three have solidified that belief and made it a reality for me."

Adrestia grabs Avyanna by the nape of the neck and swings the hunter to face her. "I fucking love you. Even after everything my family put you through to separate us, you've still chosen me in the end. I hate that it had to happen that way..." she says, trailing off to look at Roxi and me. "But you're right. If my family hadn't intervened, we wouldn't have found these two. Even if we had, I don't think things would've turned out this way. We were too lost in each other back then to allow them to enter our lives like they needed to."

Roxi shifts in my lap and brings her hand up to cup my cheek, wiping away a tear that escaped its containment. I open my mouth to apologize because I hadn't even realized she'd woken up, but she stops me with a mesmerizing smile. She looks so peaceful. Content.

I smile back at her. "Sounds like you're stuck with us. Because I wouldn't trade the way you all make me feel for anything in this entire world or the next. I've never once thought about settling down until I met you all. I'll do anything as long as it means I get to be with you three forever."

About the author

Mikaelynn Rose is a hard-working, devoted woman whose world revolves around an amazing little boy... well, I guess her husband, too. While she lives just outside of Denver with her high school sweetheart and son, she'd much rather be in the country or the mountains. When she's not working, she's writing, reading, listening to music, spending time with her loved ones, and, of course, drinking way too much coffee for her own good.

Find me on my socials!

f facebook.com/mikaelynnrose/

tiktok.com/@mikaelynnrose

tiktok.com/@author.mikaelynn.rose

instagram.com/mikaelynnrose

goodreads.com/mikaelynnrose